# A WANTED MAN

Jolly Mary was happy to see him, though she appeared to be a little worried. "Some men come here lookin' for you a little while ago," Jolly Mary said. "Five of 'em. One was a sheriff or a marshal."

"You waited long enough to tell me," Calhoun said flatly.

Jolly Mary smiled wanly. "I wanted a little time with you," she said in embarrassment.

"Well, I'd best be movin' on," Calhoun said quietly as he rose and began to dress.

"What'd you do that you got them boys after you?" Jolly Mary asked.

Calhoun just glared at her.

ALSO BY CLINT HAWKINS

**SADDLE TRAMP**
**THE CAPTIVE**
**GUNPOWDER TRAIL**
**GOLD AND LEAD**
**BANDIT'S BLOOD**
**SIOUX TRAIL**
**HORSE THIEVES' TRAIL**

Published by
HarperPaperbacks

# SADDLE TRAMP

# DEATH RIDES IN TEXAS

## CLINT HAWKINS



HarperPaperbacks
*A Division of* Harper Collins*Publishers*

HarperPaperbacks *A Division of* HarperCollins*Publishers*
10 East 53rd Street, New York, N.Y. 10022



Cover illustration by John Thompson

First printing: July 1994

Printed in the United States of America

HarperPaperbacks and colophon are trademarks of HarperCollins*Publishers*

❖ 10 9 8 7 6 5 4 3 2 1

# CHAPTER

# * 1 *

Wade Calhoun popped his head and a pistol up over the log and fired off a shot, then ducked behind the deadfall as a small fusillade of bullets slammed into the decaying wood.

"Dammit all to hell and gone," he muttered. He didn't really want to kill anyone out there, but the men of the posse seemed determined to kill him to save themselves the effort of dragging him back to West Hades and hanging him.

He had had about enough of their attempts—and of his own misguided good-heartedness. It never failed but that he got a raw deal on those rare occasions he tried to show a little decency. He ought to know better by now.

As usual, he had stumbled into trouble, rather than having walked into it. He had long ago, though, given up worrying about such things happening to him. They did, and that was all there was to it. He could either live with it, die with it, or complain about it all his life, which would do no good. Besides, Wade Calhoun was not a complaining man.

Calhoun had ridden into West Hades two days ago, looking for nothing more than a meal, a couple of drinks, a woman, and maybe a soft bed for a change. For once, he had a halfway decent horse under him and at least thirty bucks in his pockets.

West Hades was a hellhole of a little town just across the Red River from Texas, west of the Indian lands. Its buildings were ragged, and its people more so. Neither town nor residents seemed to have any purpose. The people looked beaten down, whipped by the constant wind, seared and burned by the hot summer sun, and frosted around the edges by the winters.

There were few women around, Calhoun noticed, but those few appeared to be sporting ladies, which suited him just fine. He had no intentions of looking for some fine, upstanding young woman and settling down in such a place to raise a brood of kids. This could've been the nicest city in all the West and he still would not want that. What he wanted was simple: a quick poke or two during the night. These fallen angels would fit the bill for that, even if they weren't all that much to look at.

The men seemed lean and gaunt, yet somehow soft. They shuffled about as if lost. None appeared to be threatening in any way, though most were armed. They just seemed to have lost all hope and direction. Calhoun shrugged. He wasn't interested in the men at all. Not unless some of them wanted to cause him trouble, and that appeared to be unlikely.

He stopped in front of a fetid log, sod, and adobe saloon. He knew it was a saloon since the only sign, hand painted in blue and now faded to ghostly gray, said WHISKEY 10 cent.

Calhoun dismounted and tied the buckskin horse to a rickety hitching rail. He paused, wondering if he should leave the animal alone. He wasn't all that concerned with the horse, really. Considering the luck he generally had with horses, he never formed an attachment with any of the animals he had. What did concern him, though, was his saddle. It was a Spanish-style saddle of heavy leather inlaid with designs in silver. The horn was very large, and big, fancy *tapaderos* covered the fronts of the stirrups. Two heavy Colt Walkers rode in saddle holsters, and there was a single-shot Henry in a scabbard on one side and a 10-gauge Greener double-barreled shotgun in one on the other. All in all, it would make a tempting target for any enterprising thief.

Calhoun shrugged again. No one in West Hades seemed to be the type that would try stealing his saddle. And if someone did, Calhoun would simply hunt him down and kill him. There was no question about that.

He headed into the saloon. The inside made the outside of the place look positively beauteous. It was dim, dusty, and foul smelling. The dirt floor squished when he walked on it, and he did not want to think of why it might be so wet. There was no back bar; no real bar, either, for that matter. The bar was a few small, partly planed logs that rested on a pile of wood crates on one side and an old table on the other.

The bartender was a tall, heavyset, mustachioed man who wore boldly striped pants, a frock coat, a boiled shirt, and a tie, all of which looked as if they had been left in a hog wallow for several days before he donned them. He dispensed whiskey from one barrel and beer from another. A double-barreled shotgun rested on the bar near his left hand, and he had a Colt pistol strapped to his right side, butt facing toward his middle.

"What'll it be, Mac?" the bartender asked when Calhoun stopped at the makeshift bar.

"Whiskey. And a beer." Calhoun set down a coin and pulled out his fixings and rolled a cigarette. Before lighting it, though, he lifted the small glass of whiskey, raised it in a mocking half salute toward the bartender, and swallowed it down.

It was every bit as foul as he expected it would be, but it still felt warm and comforting on the way down. He nodded and set down the glass. "Do it again," he said.

While the bartender filled the glass, Calhoun lit his cigarette. Calhoun gulped down the whiskey again and then nursed the beer while he smoked his cigarette down. Done with the beer, he thought of having another, but he decided he was hungry. He could always get another drink later.

"There someplace I can get somethin' to eat?" he asked the bartender.

"Twilley's. Five places down across the street," the man said, pointing lazily. "A hotel and dining room next to the livery."

Calhoun nodded and walked out. Behind him, he heard a commotion, then loud voices. He smoothly slipped to the side of the door, against the wall, and then peered back inside to make sure no one was coming to cause trouble for him. Several men were arguing. Calhoun shrugged. It was not his business.

He mounted his horse and headed toward the restaurant, wondering. It seemed rather odd to put a hotel and restaurant next to a stable. But he had seen worse things. A couple of gunshots rang out from the saloon behind him.

Calhoun went inside the restaurant—a dismal place that smelled of blood, burned meat, and singed fat—and ordered a beefsteak, biscuits, and coffee. He was about halfway through when he noted that a lawman had entered.

The man with the badge stopped just inside the door, looked around a moment, then headed straight for Calhoun. The man was big but flabby. His puffy-sleeved, homespun shirt was filthy and tattered, his pants had holes in the knees and seat, his boots were shabby, his vest hung lankly, and his soiled hat was crumpled. He had two pistols stuck into his belt and a cheap tin badge pinned to the vest.

The lawman shuffled up to Calhoun's table, bringing with him an air of dung and sweat and filth, and stopped. It seemed to Calhoun that a cloud of flies and gnats accompanied the man. "I'm Deputy Marshal Cole Breckenridge," the man said. "You're under arrest."

Calhoun had paused with a forkful of steak halfway to his mouth, a little surprised at Breckenridge's quiet, sonorous voice. He completed the move, then asked as he chewed, "What for?"

"Ruckus over in Flagg's saloon."

Calhoun frowned, having no clue as to what the lawman was talking about.

"A man was shot over at Flagg's just a few minutes ago. You were seen leaving there about that time."

"Flagg's? Is that the goddamn dump down the street?"

"Only saloon in West Hades," Breckenridge said. "You were there, weren't you?"

"Yep." Calhoun ate some more, though he did not feel like it. The day was turning sour, which dampened his appetite a little. Still, he kept eating, figuring there was a good chance he would need to be fortified for some action.

"A few minutes ago?"

"Just before I come here."

"Then you're under arrest." Breckenridge drew a pistol and pointed it at Calhoun, though he did not cock it.

"There's no need for that, Deputy," Calhoun said flatly, his pockmarked face slightly wrinkled with a scowl. He shoved another piece of steak into his mouth. "Let me finish my supper and I'll come along peaceably."

"You'll come along peaceably now," Breckenridge hissed. "One way or the other," he added pointedly.

Calhoun gulped down some coffee and nodded. As he started to rise, he flicked the remains of his coffee at Breckenridge.

The deputy jerked to the side and fired his pistol. The bullet went wide, and Calhoun heard someone behind him groan and fall. But he was not about to wait for Breckenridge to get off another shot.

Calhoun jerked out one of his Colt Dragoons from a cross-draw holster, thumbed back the hammer, and aimed. "Don't," he warned, figuring he ought to give Breckenridge a chance.

Breckenridge snarled and brought his own pistol up fast. He fired again, once more wide.

Calhoun did not hesitate this time. He fired twice, both lead balls punching small holes in Breckenridge's chest.

Calhoun stood there a moment, smoking pistol in hand, looking around to check out the danger, if any.

No one in the restaurant wanted to challenge this man. Calhoun was not big—about five-foot-ten and maybe 160 pounds—but his razor-thin frame belied the strength in his long, ropelike muscles. He was as hard and unyielding as a blacksmith's anvil, and standing here with that .44-caliber Dragoon in his hand he was enough to give anyone in West Hades pause.

Behind him, he noticed that three people were gathered around a woman who was sprawled on the floor, the bodice of her plain cotton dress covered with blood.

"Murderer," one of the men kneeling over the woman said, looking over his shoulder at Calhoun.

"Shit," Calhoun muttered. Such an attitude irritated him. With his left hand, he shoved another piece of steak into his mouth. Colt still in hand, he stalked out. He walked swiftly to his horse and pulled himself into the saddle, sliding the Dragoon away once he was seated. Then he spurred the horse, galloping out of West Hades, heading south.

Just outside of town, he slowed the horse, not wanting to wear the animal out. An hour later, he was swimming with his horse across the Red River, trying to make sure the powder in his weapons did not get wet. He was certain that if a posse was coming after him, the river would not stop them.

He halted on the Texas side of the river and looked back. A band of men was almost at the river. "Goddamn," he mumbled. Once more he spurred the horse into a gallop.

Riding hard, he came to a creek about two hours later. He followed it west a little way, looking for someplace to make a stand. Then he spotted a deadfall, and he decided it would do. It would have to do, since he didn't figure there was anyplace else within a reasonable distance where he could hole up for a while.

Calhoun looked over his "haven." A cottonwood had died, probably from lack of water one drought year, Calhoun figured, and had fallen down the slightly sloped, shallow bank. A few smaller trees and brush had grown up around the log and died there. Others had lived, and would provide some cover for the horse. Not that Calhoun figured the animal would live through the exchange, if it came. Not with his luck with horses. Still, it was better than nothing.

Calhoun tied the horse to some brush. He loosened the saddle some to let the animal breathe, but left it on. He wasn't sure but what he would need to be mounted and riding hard at a few moments' notice. He pulled a few pieces of beef jerky from his saddlebags and got his canteen. Then he squatted behind the log to wait. While he did, he reloaded the two chambers of the Dragoon he had used to kill Breckenridge.

He didn't have long to wait. Within half an hour, the posse rode into sight. Calhoun sat patiently, hoping that the posse would miss him, cross the creek, and keep on riding.

The men almost did, but as they crossed the creek thirty yards west of Calhoun, one of the posse men glanced in his direction and apparently saw his horse. He stopped and shouted to the others, pointing.

Calhoun shot him out of the saddle. He got one more before the six others had managed to find shelter amid the sparse cover along the creek. All but one of their horses ran off.

One posse member sprinted across the creek and began edging up toward Calhoun's position, but Calhoun shot him dead, too. Calhoun figured that would keep the other men put, at least for a while.

# CHAPTER

# * 2 *

Calhoun realized he was in a tight spot, though, as the day wore on. Still outnumbered five to one, he couldn't hope to hold out all night. As soon as it got dark, he figured, the men of the posse would start moving in on him. At best, they would simply shoot his horse and wait for him to try to get away on foot. Then he would be at their mercy, or so he figured they would think. They might be surprised, though, he knew. At worst, they would simply overrun his position and gun him down without a second thought. There was almost no chance they would want to drag him back to West Hades just to hang him.

"This is West Hades Marshal Russ Conroy," a man shouted sometime during that long, blistering hot afternoon. "You're in one heap of goddamn trouble, boy, and you'd do yourself well to give yourself up now."

"For what, a lynchin'?" Calhoun countered.

"You'll get a fair trial."

"And then a fair hangin'," someone else said.

"Go to hell, Marshal," Calhoun said calmly.

"Things're gonna go hard on y'all, boy," Conroy said. "It weren't bad enough y'all went and kilt Deputy Breckenridge, but you had to go and kill three of my men here. That weren't right."

"I could've killed a couple more before you boys got under cover," Calhoun said. "But I didn't." He figured that his benevolence would do him absolutely no good at all. Still, he had no real desire to kill any more of these men, not unless it was necessary.

On the other hand, surrendering and going to meet his Maker did have some attraction for him. He had been trying to get himself killed ever since the Sioux had raided his farm in Kansas Territory. The thought of his dear Lizbeth and their darling infant Lottie being slaughtered filled him with a combination of rage and deep despair. He often thought of what it would be like to be with Lizbeth and Lottie again in the hereafter.

There were two problems with that idea, though. For one thing, his survival instincts were so strongly ingrained that they would not allow him to just give up and die. The second was the more troublesome to him, though: While he knew for sure that Lizbeth and Lottie were in heaven—if indeed there were a heaven—he was pretty well certain that there was no way the good Lord would allow him into His holy kingdom. Not with the way he had lived his life. So to just give up and march to an early death would do him no good.

Throughout the sporadic gunfire he and the posse exchanged during the blazing hot day, Calhoun pondered what he should do. But when he really came down to it, there were only two choices. He could beat the posse men at their own game, sneaking up on them as soon as it was dark and killing them; or he could take off and hope to outrun them. He could not wait them out, that was the one thing that was certain.

Normally, his choice would be easy. He generally had such a poor excuse for a horse that outrunning a posse would be virtually impossible. But he had lucked out with this strong young buckskin mare. Still, considering his luck with horses, he was a little reluctant to try outrunning the posse. The way things usually went for him, the horse would break its neck somehow and leave him afoot out in the middle of the prairie with no cover.

Then he quit worrying about it. There had been enough killing for one day, even for a man whose life was so immersed in bloodshed. Not that he would shy away from more, if the need arose. He just figured it was time to cut and run.

Just as dusk was giving way to darkness, Calhoun slid down the mucky bank and began to talk quietly to his horse, hoping the animal would make no noise. He tightened the saddle and then walked the horse across the creek. He continued to walk southeast, towing the horse behind him for a few dozen yards. Then he flung himself into the saddle and spurred the horse into a run.

Calhoun let the horse go as long as he could. The animal surprised him with its stamina. Finally, though, somewhere along in the night, Calhoun slowed the horse, and eventually he stopped. He loosened the saddle and then moved a little away from the horse. If the posse was chasing him, he should be able to hear it on a quiet, calm night like this. Especially since the wind was blowing lightly from the posse's direction.

Throughout the night and all the next day, Calhoun kept riding at a fairly slow pace, stopping only for five or ten minutes every hour to give the horse a short break. He skirted two towns, figuring they were still too close to West Hades.

By dusk of the next day, though, he figured he had come nearly sixty miles, and when he spotted another town, he rode in. He was hot, dusty, tired, and more than a little irritable.

Finding the livery was easy—he just followed the familiar stench. The owner, an irascible old man named Barney Philpot, was just about ready to close up for the day, and was not happy when Calhoun rode into the corral.

"Five dollars change your attitude any?" Calhoun asked as he unsaddled the buckskin.

Philpot nodded, eyes eager for the money.

"Grain her good. She's been hard used. Make sure she gets plenty of water and a good groomin'."

"I know my business, mister," Philpot snapped.

"You better," Calhoun answered in kind. "There a hotel in town?"

"Down yonder street," Philpot said, pointing. "About halfway. On the left."

Calhoun nodded. "They got eats there?"

"Old lady Kohl serves a decent steak."

Calhoun nodded again. He flipped a five-dollar gold piece to Philpot. Then, carrying his saddle over his left shoulder, he strolled off. He found the Kohls' place without trouble, got himself a small room, dropped the saddle off, and then headed for the dining room. He packed away a fair amount of groceries and coffee before leaning back and rolling a cigarette.

He realized his eyes were gritty with tiredness and trail dust, so as soon as he finished the cigarette, he went to his room. He was asleep within moments of his head hitting the lumpy down pillow.

Calhoun ate well in the morning, too, then headed toward the livery to check on his horse. On the walk, he checked out the town. He decided that Nettleville was a dingy little town with delusions of grandiosity. On the outside, it looked a lot better than West Hades, but inside, it was much the same—poor buildings inhabited by worn businessmen, tradesmen, and families. There were few amenities in the town, and most families that he could see would not have been able to afford them anyway.

The buckskin had been well taken care of, and looked rested. Calhoun nodded and headed back up the street, eyes searching for a saloon. He had no intention of staying in Nettleville long, but he was still annoyed that he had been run out of West Hades before enjoying the companionship of a fallen angel. He intended to rectify that before he pulled out of Nettleville.

At the first saloon he found, a dismal little place

that fit his mood just fine, he had three shots of poor whiskey and a mug of warm, flat beer. Then he left.

On the way to the saloon, he had seen a brothel, and when he left the bar, he headed for the bawdy house. It was one of the few plank buildings in Nettleville, and it seriously needed a coat of paint on the outside. It also had several loose boards that snapped and flapped in the wind. The three stairs to the small porch creaked from overuse, and the door did not close properly. Not that he cared.

A short, chubby, shabbily dressed man met Calhoun just inside. "Name's Red. I own this place," the man announced.

Calhoun shrugged, looking past Red to the six women standing on the stairway behind the pimp. None looked particularly appealing, but one he saw was at least bearable to look at. He pointed to her. "How much for that brown-haired 'beauty' there?" he asked.

"Two bucks. For any of 'em." Red never looked to where Calhoun was pointing. "How long you gonna be?"

"Till I'm done," Calhoun said flatly.

Several of the girls giggled.

Red did not. He looked like he had just swallowed a mouthful of castor oil. He was an unpleasant looking—and smelling—man who, though only in his late twenties, was pretty well bald. What hair he did have was greasy and hung lankly.

Calhoun knew he looked little better, as far as cleanliness and grooming went. He hadn't shaved in some days, and he was covered with trail dust and sweat. His hair, as usual, was fairly long and scruffy looking. His clothes were dirty and quite worn.

"That ain't much funny, y'all," Red said sourly.

Calhoun shrugged. He shoved past Red, heading for the women.

"Hey, goddammit, where'n the hell're you goin'?" Red asked angrily, turning.

Calhoun stopped and looked back. He pointed upstairs.

"Not without you payin' me first you ain't," Red said adamantly, pudgy face determined.

"I'll pay when I leave," Calhoun said calmly.

"Like hell you will. You pay me now, or you go mosey on out, friend."

Calhoun scowled a little. He pulled a ten-dollar gold piece of out his pocket and threw it on the floor at Red's feet. "I might even come get some change," he said quietly.

"Don't push your luck with me, friend," Red snapped.

"You're gonna make me tremble," Calhoun said. "And that might upset all these here ladies." He turned, and pointed to the one he wanted. "After you, ma'am," he said. Then he followed the woman up the stairs.

It was almost dark when he finally felt like leaving. Jolly Mary hadn't minded, especially when Calhoun had ordered them lunch, and later supper, in the room.

"No change needed, lard ass," Calhoun said to Red as he headed out. Had he been a smiling man, he would have favored the pimp with a grin.

Calhoun went back to the saloon, had a few whiskeys, and then went to his room.

In the morning, Calhoun was a little reluctant to leave Nettleville just yet, so after eating, he went to the saloon again, where he drank and gambled the morning away. After another meal, he shrugged and headed for Red's once more.

Red seemed mighty edgy, but Calhoun shrugged it off. Red seemed the type to be edgy most of the time.

Jolly Mary was happy to see him, though she appeared to be a little worried. When Calhoun and she were finished, he asked about it. He didn't care all that much, but he was a little concerned that Red might be irritated at her because of something he had done.

"Some men come here lookin' for you a little while ago," Jolly Mary said. "Five of 'em. One was a sheriff or a marshal."

"You waited long enough to tell me," Calhoun said flatly.

Jolly Mary smiled wanly. "I wanted a little time with you," she said in embarrassment.

"Well, I'd best be movin' on," Calhoun said quietly as he rose and began to dress.

"What'd you do that you got them boys after you?" Jolly Mary asked.

Calhoun just glared at her and finished dressing. As he headed out the door, he realized that the visit by the posse probably was what had Red so edgy.

The pimp stuck his head out of a room as Calhoun came downstairs. Calhoun suddenly grabbed him, hauled him into the small hallway, and slammed him up against a wall. "You sent someone to find that goddamn posse and bring 'em back here, didn't you?" he demanded.

"I don't know what you're talkin' about, friend," Red said unctuously.

"You don't? Well, Mister Red, just think about this: I killed the deputy marshal over in West Hades. Then I killed three of them in the posse that's chasin' me."

Red almost wet his pants. He did not need Calhoun to explain that he would not think twice before killing Red if it seemed the right thing to do at the time. He also realized how close he had come to getting killed by Calhoun last night.

Calhoun released him. "You treat these ladies right, you hear? Or I'll come pay you a visit." Then he walked out.

Calhoun walked swiftly, but not overly so, to the hotel. Along the way, he saw the posse men's horses outside another restaurant. He moved on by and went to his hotel. In minutes he had packed his few belongings in his saddlebags, hefted his saddle over his left shoulder, and headed outside again.

Barney Philpot was a little surprised to see him, but Calhoun did not explain why he was there. He simply saddled the buckskin and left. He stopped at the only general store in Nettleville, bought a few supplies, and then rode slowly out of town, heading mostly south. He wondered how long it would be before the posse was back on his trail.

# CHAPTER

# ★ 3 ★

Calhoun rode hard once again, and was surprised when he spotted the lights of another town just after dark. He rode around it and kept on going. There was plenty of light from the fat, almost full moon.

By midway through the next day, he came to still another town, this one perhaps thirty-five miles from the one he had skipped. He decided to pull into town for a meal and to get some more supplies. He had been in a hurry to leave Nettleville, and so had purchased little in the way of provisions.

He stopped at the Grassdale livery to allow the men there to feed, water, and groom the buckskin, while he went to the first restaurant he found. He ate a good portion of passable chicken with yams and corn bread, coffee, and pecan pie. Then he wandered to a general store and picked up some supplies, though he could not carry much. Still, between that and the livery, he was down to nine dollars and eighty-seven cents.

He rode out of Grassdale an hour and a half after he rode in. He was annoyed at still being on the run, and vowed that if the posse caught up to him again, he would make a stand and put an end to it.

Calhoun continued traveling south, and two days later he was in the hill country of central Texas. That was about the time he spotted the posse on his trail again. He stopped on a ridge and watched them for a bit. The five men were only a mile or so back. He had no reaction when someone in the posse saw him and pointed.

As the men of the posse began galloping toward him, Calhoun turned his horse and walked it down the far side. From up on the ridge, he had seen a small stand of trees surrounding a spring several miles off. He had vowed to fight off the posse, but he was not foolish enough to want to do so out in the open when cover was not far off. If he could make the stand of trees, he would have a good chance of taking care of all the men in the posse.

At the bottom of the grassy knoll, he trotted off. Occasionally he would look back, not really expecting to see the posse for a while. But they came up behind him a lot faster than he had figured. When they saw Calhoun, they got a little more speed out of their horses.

Calhoun shook his head in annoyance. Being cocky had gotten him in trouble before, and it looked like it was about to happen again. He spurred the horse until it was going full out.

He was thundering along, fully confident that he

was easily going to outdistance his pursuers, when the buckskin's right front foreleg hit a chuckhole and snapped.

Calhoun went sailing as the horse screamed and skidded along on its chest. Calhoun landed hard on his left side, then bounced and rolled, banging head, knees, elbows, and chin on the scrubby grass. He finally came to a stop ten yards beyond the horse.

"Goddamn," Calhoun breathed as he lay there a minute. He was a little stunned from the landing, but he was aware enough to be surprised when he realized that none of his bones seemed to be broken. Hearing the horse's pained whinnying, Calhoun rolled over and pushed himself onto his hands and knees. He would know for sure soon enough if he had broken anything or not.

He stood, weaving, and then lurched off. He got a little dizzy when he straightened back up after bending to retrieve his hat, and it took some moments for him to clear the cobwebs out of his head.

He headed with an unsteady gait toward the horse. The animal was standing on three legs, seemingly wondering why its fourth leg didn't work. Calhoun shook his head in annoyance. He should have known, he thought. He managed to get the saddle off the buckskin, and then he shot the animal in the head, dancing out of the way as the beast fell.

Angry, Calhoun flopped down behind the horse after it had ceased jerking in death. He pulled his single-shot rifle and his two big Walker pistols. He had just about done that when the posse rode into view over a small hill a hundred yards off.

Calhoun fired the rifle, and one of the pursuers

fell. Since the posse was still coming on hard, Calhoun had no time to reload his rifle. He grabbed a Walker and waited until the pursuers were a little closer. When they were fifty yards away, he began firing.

The last three posse men pulled up sharply when another of their men went down under Calhoun's gunfire.

Calhoun took out one more before the remaining two got into prone positions on the ground and started firing back. Bullets smacked into the buckskin's carcass with loud, bloody splats. The posse men's horses fled back the way they came. The men figured it was better to stay out of the line of fire than to worry about the horses. If they got killed, the horses wouldn't matter. If they took Calhoun, they were certain they could round up the animals again.

Not being able to really see the two remaining posse men any longer, Calhoun rolled onto his back and patiently reloaded his rifle and the two Walkers. By the time he had finished, the gunfire from his pursuers had stopped. He figured they were waiting for him to make some kind of move, though he knew they might be out there thinking they had killed him.

Calhoun shoved one of the Walkers into his belt in the back. Rolling back onto his stomach, he began crawling to his right, moving slowly and carefully. The grass here was not very tall and he had no intention of ending up shot in the buttocks or something because it was up in the air. Nor did he want to be seen. He was hoping the two men might eventually come looking to see if they had killed him. If they did, he would be ready for them.

He estimated the temperature was at least 103. The sun was unmerciful, beating down with a vicious intensity. It seemed to Calhoun after a few minutes that the sun was trying to fry him into a little puddle, and was doing so with malicious glee. Sweat rolled off his face and also drenched the front and back of his shirt.

Calhoun finally quit slinking along, and stopped. He worked his legs around so that he was lying prone, facing where he had last seen the two posse men. Once more he waited. That and the almost unbearable heat did little to improve his humor.

Within half an hour he realized he had been a fool for not bringing his canteen with him when he had moved away from the horse. He was thirsty already, and knew it would only get worse. An hour later, his tongue had begun to swell a little.

"Shit," he muttered, trying to work up a little moisture into his dry mouth. He picked up a pebble and put it in his mouth. That helped some, but he was still annoyed at himself—and at the posse men who were responsible for his being here this way.

Finally he had had enough of the waiting. He set his rifle down and pulled the second Walker out of his belt. Then he began crawling again, this time heading for where he had last seen his two foes. He moved a little faster and a bit less cautiously than he had before. His thirst was great enough that he cared less now about being seen.

When he thought he was within fifteen feet or so of the men, he stopped and took a breather. He was beginning to think that his foes, too, had moved, until he suddenly heard a whispered, "Wonder where that son of a bitch is."

"Out there," came the reply in kind.

If Calhoun had been the kind of man to grin in victory, he would've done so then. Silently and carefully he checked both big pistols, hoping he had not sweated on them and dampened the powder. They appeared to be all right. He figured that in any case, his two Dragoons, worn on his hips in cross-draw holsters, would be all right.

Calhoun crawled a few more feet forward, inching along so as not to make any sound or raise any dust. He suddenly stood straight up, cocking the Walkers as he did.

The two posse men—one of them West Hades Marshal Russ Conroy—had no chance. Conroy tried to do something, though, rolling as hard and fast as he could toward Calhoun. He fired once as soon as he came to a stop, but then he felt lead balls puncture his throat, cracking his trachea and larynx; tear into his chest and through a lung; and snap the bone in his right upper arm.

Conroy had reacted so quickly that Calhoun's first shot had missed. Rather than try to hit a moving target, Calhoun had swung toward the other posse man. Two shots squeezed off with the Walker in his left hand had taken care of him. Then Calhoun had turned his attention back to Conroy, and fired smoothly.

Calhoun knelt next to the lawman. "You and your boys should've stayed back in West Hades," Calhoun said quietly.

Conroy tried to say something, but his fractured larynx would not allow it. All that came out was a pained, wheezing sound.

There was no sign of fear in the lawman's eyes, though, and Calhoun respected that. Because of it, Calhoun figured the man deserved some sort of explanation. "I didn't have nothin' to do with that saloon fight back there," he said.

Conroy's eyes raised in surprise.

"I heard some shootin' just after I left the saloon. If that goddamn stupid deputy of yours would've listened to me, you wouldn't be layin' here dyin'."

Conroy hesitated only a moment, then nodded. He winced as pain stabbed at his neck and chest. Then he tensed, and the light faded from his eyes.

"Damn fool," Calhoun said, not sure whether he was talking to Conroy or himself. He closed the lawman's eyes and stood. He took the nearest canteen he found—the only one within sight—and drank deeply of the lukewarm, stagnant water. It tasted delicious.

Thirst slaked, he checked the four other men just to make sure. All were dead. He went through each man's pockets, pulling out what money he found. When he was done, he had the grand total—including his own nine dollars and change—of eighteen dollars and fifty-four cents. He thought it odd that the posse men had so little money, until he realized they had been on his trail for some days and must have had to buy supplies at least once or twice.

Calhoun went and retrieved his rifle and put it by his saddle. Then he stood and smoked a cigarette while he pondered his immediate future. He had little money, no horse, and he was, as far as he knew, miles from the nearest town. Things were about usual for him. He figured he ought to bury the posse men—at least the marshal. The lawman deserved that much. But he had no shovel and it was still hotter than blazes.

"Ah, shit," he mumbled as he crushed out the cigarette under a boot heel. He headed toward Conroy's body and took the lawman's big knife. Finding a relatively soft spot a few feet away, he began hacking at the earth with the knife.

Within minutes Calhoun was drenched in sweat, but still he persevered, until he had a shallow hole big enough to accommodate the fair-sized marshal. He grabbed Conroy's belt and half carried, half dragged him to the hole and dropped him in it. Then he kicked the dirt over the lawman and stomped it down.

Calhoun walked back to his dead horse and sat on it, much to the annoyance of the swarms of flies that had found this succulent treat. He rolled a cigarette and lit it. He ached all over after having taken such a tumble from his horse. Crawling around hadn't helped much, nor had digging the grave. He was a little shaky, too, from hunger, overexertion, and heat.

With a sigh, he crushed out the cigarette and stood. Pulling the Walkers from his belt, he put them back in the saddle holsters. He put the rifle away, too, then hauled the saddle up onto his shoulder and shuffled off.

It didn't take long to get to the small stand of trees he had been trying to make when the horse went down. He set the saddle down and then gathered firewood and made a small blaze. He looked at his supplies, and realized he was pretty low on everything. He filled his little coffeepot and set it on the fire, then wearily trudged back to his dead horse.

With a healthy dose of distaste, he hacked some meat from the carcass, then plodded back to his fire. The horse meat tasted as bad as he knew it would, but it gave him some strength. After finishing a fair portion of it, plus two cups of coffee and another cigarette, he was feeling almost human again.

So comfortable was he that he was set to spend the night where he was, but then he decided that might not be the best idea. He had no idea where he really was or how far it was to a town or anything. Traveling at night would be far better.

Plus there was one more cup's worth of coffee in the pot, so he nursed that as he cleaned, oiled, and reloaded all his weapons, including his backup pistol—a Colt Walker with the barrel cut down to about two inches. He carried the nasty looking weapon in a holster at the small of his back under his shirt, and the powder in it had become soaked with sweat.

By the time he finished, it was just about dark, and to his relief the temperature was already down a few degrees. He kicked dirt over the fire, stowed away his coffeepot, and then hauled his saddle up onto his shoulder. He was pleased to feel a refreshing breeze as he moved out of the trees.

He traveled until almost daylight, when he found another small stand of trees around a spring. There was hardly any water in the spring, but it was far better than nothing. He slept the day away and then walked on again once darkness came. The next day he was out in the open, and slept poorly as the sun's unbearable heat smashed down on him.

Calhoun went through another night of walking. Not finding a suitable place to stop, he kept on walking, figuring he'd better get to water soon. As he topped another small, grassy hill, he spotted two parallel lines of trees—and a farmhouse.

# CHAPTER

# * 4 *

Calhoun walked down the lane formed by the two rows of trees. He stopped near the small, neat frame house and set down the heavy saddle. He pulled off his hat and wiped a sleeve across his sweating brow.

A tall, powerfully built man came out of the small barn nearby. He walked toward Calhoun, gazing at him in curiosity.

The front door of the house opened, and a short, pudgy woman stepped out onto the small porch, wiping her hands on her apron.

As the two people neared him, Calhoun noticed that they were elderly. Probably in their sixties, Calhoun figured. Both were gray haired but looked strong and healthy.

"Somethin' I can do for you, mister?" the man asked. He was not nervous, despite having gotten a good look at Calhoun's hard face and his armaments.

"I'm kind of short on cash," Calhoun said, hating himself for begging, as he saw it. "I was wonderin' if you maybe had some chores I could do in return for some money." The eighteen-plus dollars he had was not nearly enough to buy a horse and supplies. With a meal or two—and maybe even a stake of a few more dollars—he could head for the nearest town and take enough work to set himself up with a horse.

"You don't look like no farmhand to me."

"I ain't," Calhoun said sourly. "But I'm strong and willin' to work."

"Mother?" the man asked the woman.

"You look like a hardcase, mister," the woman said, squinting at Calhoun.

He shrugged. He reached into a shirt pocket and pulled out his fixings. "There's been times I've been called on to be such, ma'am," he said quietly as he rolled a cigarette.

"I expect that's been true more often than it ain't," the woman said.

Calhoun nodded. He saw no need to respond further to that.

"How come you to be down-and-out?"

"Always had trouble with horses, ma'am," Calhoun said with another shrug. "I was chasing a buffalo when my mare stepped in a chuckhole. Tossed me bottom side over teakettle. I've been walkin' the past few days."

The woman looked at him sharply. "I do believe, sir, that there's a heap more to what's gone on than you're lettin' on here."

"Might be, ma'am," Calhoun said flatly.

"You look hungry, boy," she said.

"I could do with a bite."

"My name's Millie Fuller. My husband's Jess." She stopped and waited.

"Wade Calhoun, ma'am."

Millie nodded. "Put your saddle in the barn over there and then wash up around back. The table'll be set by the time you're done with that."

"Yes'm. I'm obliged." He dropped the cigarette butt and stomped it out. Then he hoisted the saddle again and shuffled off. He dropped the saddle inside an empty stall in the barn and took a few moments to look around. There were two milch cows and four big mules in other stalls. Chickens scratched around for corn.

After a moment's thought, Calhoun bent and pulled his straight razor, shaving soap, and mug from his saddlebags. In back of the house he found a pump and a basin. A fresh piece of soft cloth was draped over the pump handle, and a cake of lye soap sat in the basin.

After taking the soap out and setting it down, Calhoun pumped water into the basin and then worked up some lather for shaving. He hacked off the growth on his face quickly, heedless of the cuts he knew he was inflicting on himself. Then he pulled off his shirt and washed himself up as well as he could. The lye soap stung the fresh cuts on his face, and even the crusted-over ones he had gotten when he had been flung off his horse. Finally he dumped the basin out, dried off, and put his shirt on. Then he knocked on the back door of the house.

Millie Fuller let him in, smiling warmly when she

saw his scraped, raw face. Cleaned up, she thought, he wasn't an unhandsome man, despite some pocking of the face and the hard, flat look in his eyes.

Calhoun sat at the table, returning Jess Fuller's nod. He started to reach for some food, but stopped at Millie's sharp voice.

"We might be out here on the far edge of nowhere, Mister Calhoun," she said gruffly, "and we might not get to church but a few times a year, but we do say grace before our meals."

Calhoun nodded and leaned back. He waited more or less patiently as Fuller said grace. Then Millie nodded at him, and Calhoun dug in.

The Fullers, despite still being wary of Calhoun, were rather amused at the amount of food the saddle tramp packed away. When Calhoun finally leaned back and rolled a cigarette, Fuller said, "When's the last time you ate, boy?" He was smiling.

"Couple, three days, I guess, since I had a real meal, and that was horse meat. I can't abide horse meat."

"Especially when it's your own horse, eh?" Fuller said with a burly laugh.

Calhoun shrugged. "I never have a horse long enough to get fond of it, if that's what you mean," he offered. "But this one was better than most I've had."

"What do you usually do with yourself, Mister Calhoun?" Fuller asked.

Calhoun shrugged again.

"You a bandit, boy?" Fuller was not afraid of Calhoun. He was too old to care about dying. He and Millie had faced all manner of dangers in the thirty-plus years they had been out here, and they had weathered them all pretty well. "Or maybe a border ruffian?"

"Nope. Just a drifter."

"A man your age ought to have a wife and family."

Calhoun felt as if he had been stabbed in the guts. A vision of a burning Kansas Territory farmstead flickered before his eyes, giving way to the picture of two broken, bloody bodies. He shoved up from the table. "I'm obliged for your kindness. I'll be at your disposal in the mornin'."

"Sit down, boy," Fuller snapped. When a surprised—and suddenly angry—Calhoun did so, Fuller added, "You ain't the first man lost family. What was it? Pox? Cholera? Indians?" He could tell from the look on Calhoun's face that the last guess had been correct.

"We lost a baby boy to the Comanches more'n twenty-five years ago," Fuller said. "Lost a girl to cholera a few years before that. My brother's family was wiped out by the Comanches. Every damn one of them was butchered." Old anger, steeped in years of memory, had crept into his voice.

Calhoun said nothing, just sat with pain and hate etched on his face.

"And what's your story, Mister Calhoun?" Fuller asked quietly, back to normal.

Calhoun shrugged, jaw tight.

"Comanches?" Fuller asked. "Pawnee? Apache?"

"Sioux," Calhoun snapped. "Up in Kansas Territory."

"And so you just give up on life, is that it, boy?" Fuller demanded.

"It was my fault," Calhoun said, voice filled with self-loathing.

"Ah, I see," Fuller said sarcastically, "so you're the only man ever to lead his family into danger, and then not be able to get them out. That it, boy?"

Rage burned in Calhoun's eyes, and one hand edged toward a Dragoon. He had killed men for far less serious insults; he would have no qualms about killing Jess Fuller for this one. But he could see no fear in the old man, and he realized that Fuller was the first man he had met in a long time who was as hardheaded and fearless as he himself. He also realized that Fuller's sarcasm was well placed in this case. Many was the man who had been dealt such a blow by life, but few of them turned into an angry, violent man who lived his life disconnected from the rest of humanity. He didn't know why he couldn't be like those others. All he knew was that he was the way he was, and he accepted it.

Calhoun moved his hands back to the tabletop, and he nodded once curtly. "You got a point," he said tightly.

"I thought so. Now if I was y'all, I'd—"

"I said you got a point," Calhoun interrupted, voice harsh. "Don't push it."

"He's right, Jess," Millie interjected. She was suddenly afraid. Not for herself, but for her husband. She knew he had no fear of dying, but she did not know what she would do without him. And she had seen her husband's death in Calhoun's eyes, sure as anything. She wanted to wait as long as possible before she became a widow. "Such things're none of our beeswax."

"But, Mother . . ."

"Mister Calhoun's a guest in our house, Father. He shouldn't be lambasted with prying questions." She turned toward Calhoun and smiled in a matronly way. "Mister Fuller forgets his manners at times, Mister Calhoun," she said quietly. "You see, we don't get many visitors out here."

She was still smiling, but Calhoun could see the hurt in her. "No children, ma'am?" he asked.

"All of 'em've either died or moved on to make their own way."

"I'm sorry." He wasn't really, but he did feel a little sympathy for the old woman. "No town nearby?"

"Pecan Grove. Half a day's ride southwest. We don't get there too often. Just once in a while to bring in some crops or to get supplies. But we can't say as we know many folks there anymore. None of 'em enough to have 'em come visitin', except for Preacher Maughm, and he only gets out here once in a blue moon, what with all the other invitations he gets. And we know some of the folks who've been here a long time like Mister Fuller and me. But, like us, they're a little long in the tooth for much visitin'."

Calhoun nodded. "I ain't much on manners myself, ma'am," he said. "Such things do get rusty when you don't often use 'em. Especially for those of us who didn't maybe have many to start with." He stared at Fuller.

The old man smiled just a little. "Some folks just don't take to such things right from an early age," he offered by way of apology. "Nor at a later age, despite some others' constant efforts. Right, Mother?"

"I declare, I've been after him since before we was wedded to change his ways, but it's not taken hold in him, even after all these years." Millie sighed.

"Don't keep you from still tryin' to teach this old dog some new tricks, though, does it, Mother?" Fuller said with a laugh.

"Land's sake, no! I'll be after you till the day you breathe your last, Jess Fuller, and don't you ever doubt it."

Calhoun was glad the conversation had taken a lighter tone. Not that he was a man who enjoyed lightheartedness, but he didn't want to sit here sparring with these two people. They had been, all in all, kind to him so far.

"More coffee, Mister Calhoun?" Millie asked.

"No, ma'am. I've had my fill." He rose. "I think it's time I got some sleep. It all right if I bed down in the barn? Or would you rather have me stay out in the open somewhere?"

"A mite early for beddin' down for one so young, ain't it, boy?" Fuller countered.

Calhoun shrugged.

"Oh, leave him be, Jess," Millie said. "He's had many a day on foot, and he's probably tired." She smiled at her husband, and then at Calhoun. "The barn's fine," she said. "There's plenty of fresh straw. Make yourself comfortable."

"We rise early around here," Fuller added.

"You come get me if I ain't up," Calhoun said flatly.

"I'll do that."

Calhoun shook his head, partly in annoyance, partly at Fuller's sheer pigheadedness, and turned for the barn. Once there, he forked a decent pile of hay in the stall where he had his saddle, then spread out his bedroll. Finally he stretched out on his blankets, grateful for the comfort of the hay under him. He was still sore all over from being thrown by the horse. The several days of walking hadn't helped much either.

As he lay there a few minutes listening to the sounds of the cows, mules, and chickens and the pigs out behind the barn, he wondered what he would do next. He figured he owed the Fullers at least a full day's work for today's meal, plus those he would get tomorrow. He wondered how long they would let him stay on. He didn't relish farming—never had—and he had no intention of staying here too long. The Fullers didn't look like the type to have much money, so he didn't hold out too much hope of getting the cash here to buy a horse.

He figured he would spend no more than a day or two here before heading into Pecan Grove. Perhaps he could find a job there that would allow him to save enough in a short time to buy a horse. Then he could get on the move again, though for where, he had no idea.

It wasn't great, but at least it was some kind of plan. Satisfied with it for now, he closed his eyes and fell asleep.

# CHAPTER

# ★ 5 ★

"Land's sake, you're a mess, Mister Calhoun," Millie Fuller said. She stood with a pitcher of water, looking at Calhoun, who was not wearing his shirt.

Calhoun stopped digging the small irrigation ditch from the creek and stuck the long-handled shovel into a pile of dirt. He looked at Millie evenly. "I told you I got thrown from my horse, ma'am," he said quietly.

"That's right, Mother, he did," Fuller said from nearby. He, too, stopped working and was wiping the sweat off his brow with a large, sopping bandanna.

"You didn't get those from being thrown from no horse, Mister Calhoun," Millie said, pointing at the several old bullet holes and knife scars on Calhoun's torso.

"Perhaps not, ma'am." He paused. "If such a sight is troublin' to you . . ." He reached for his shirt.

"That's not necessary," Millie said evenly. "Here, have some water."

As Calhoun took the pitcher and drank, Fuller moved a little closer to Calhoun. Then he whistled. "Good Lord, boy," he said, "Mother's right, you are a mess. Damn, you're some hell-raiser, ain't you."

Calhoun wasn't sure whether Fuller was impressed or disgusted. "I suppose," he allowed.

"Must be with all them—"

"That's enough now, Jess," Millie scolded. "Mister Calhoun's worked hard for us these past two days."

"That he has," Fuller agreed. He had been a little surprised at how hard Calhoun worked. Fuller knew the saddle tramp would never make a farmer, but a man couldn't accuse Calhoun of being a slacker.

"Then there's no need to subject him to your disrespectful comments and such."

"Sorry, Mother." Fuller took the pitcher from Calhoun and grinned. He looked puzzled when the smile was not returned.

Millie shook her head. She could see that Calhoun was not a smiling man, and it made her a little sad that someone would not have that capability. She took the pitcher from her husband and turned back toward the house.

After two more days of working around the farm—mainly plowing a new section of land for the Fullers, an abominable job when done with a single mule—Calhoun felt the need to push on. But there was no way he could pull out, since he still had no real money. He decided he would head to Pecan

Grove, have himself a small spree, and check out the possibilities there.

"That's a fine idea," Millie said when Calhoun announced that he was going into Pecan Grove. "A young man needs some time in the city."

Calhoun nodded. "Anything I can get for you while I'm there, ma'am?"

"I couldn't expect you to . . ."

"Unless it's somethin' that ain't to be mentioned in mixed company, ma'am, I can buy or get whatever you need."

"But you've done so much for us already."

"Ain't been much. And you and Mister Fuller've been more'n fair and kind to me."

"Well, we could use some flour and coffee and . . ."

"Best make him up a list, Mother."

Millie nodded and went to do so, leaving the two men at the table, where they had just finished their noon meal.

"I'd be obliged if you'd take in a wagonload of wheat to the mill, Wade," Fuller said.

Calhoun nodded.

Fuller chewed on his lower lip a few minutes before shrugging and asking, "How're me and Mother to know you'll be back, Mister Calhoun?"

"Because I give you my word."

Fuller looked skeptical.

"My saddle's still out in the barn. You think I'd just up and leave it?"

"No. No, sir, I reckon you wouldn't at that." Fuller was still a little uncertain but felt somewhat better about it all.

Millie returned a few minutes later with a piece of

paper and an armful of clothes. "You can't go into Pecan Grove lookin' like such a fright, Mister Calhoun," she said. "These clothes're old but they're still serviceable. They belonged to our son Michael, who's moved off to Californy."

"Thank you, ma'am."

"If you want to give yourself a good scrubbin' over in the creek, I'll stay inside the house here so you can have some privacy."

"That'd be good, ma'am. Thank you." He rose and took the clothes. "Keep your list till later, Miz Fuller. I'll come by before I leave and get it."

Millie nodded, and Calhoun left. Fuller followed him. "I'll hitch the team to the wagon while you wash up, Wade," the old man said.

"Reckon I'll help," Calhoun responded. "And I'll help you load it, too. Once that's done I can clean up."

Fuller nodded, and the two men went straight to work after Calhoun dropped the clothes off on his bedroll. It did not take them long, and soon Calhoun was trudging down to a clear spot in the creek. Half an hour later, Calhoun had Millie's list—plus ten of her hard-won dollars—in a pocket and was wheeling toward Pecan Grove.

The journey took most of the afternoon, but dusk was still a few hours off when he rode into town. He drove straight to the mill and had the men there unload the wheat.

The mill owner, Steve Tanner, looked at Calhoun a little suspiciously. It was not like the Fullers to send someone else—and a stranger to boot—into town on an errand like this, he thought before realizing that if Calhoun had done something to the Fullers, he certainly wouldn't have ridden into Pecan Grove with a load of wheat to be milled. "I'll take two bags of flour as payment," he said.

Calhoun nodded. "Miz Fuller said that was usual. I'll be back sometime tomorrow to pick up the flour." He left and drove to the nearest livery, one of two in town, and dropped off the wagon and team of mules. Next he found a saloon—a properly disreputable looking place—where he had two whiskeys and a beer. Then he left to get something to eat.

Millie had told him to eat at Knowlton's, so that's where he went. It was good food and plentiful, but Calhoun had become spoiled by Millie's delicious and filling meals. Still, it was tasty enough and filled him well. He wandered back toward the saloon, Hanney's.

Pecan Grove seemed a pleasant little place. Most of the buildings were made of planks, with shake roofs. All seemed neat and trim and in good repair—quite unlike West Hades, he noted. It seemed a decent place to start a family. As such, he was beginning to dislike it already.

In Hanney's, he ordered a shot of rye and a beer and sat at a table by himself. He watched for a while as working girls took men to the several rooms on the second floor of the saloon. Most of the girls weren't much to look at, but there was one who seemed to have a certain forlorn sexiness about her that set her a little apart from all the others.

Calhoun rejected the advances of three working girls, until the one he had had his eye on showed up at his table.

"My friends tell me you've turned them down," she said with a noticeable German accent. "There somethink wrong vit' you?"

"Nope. I was just waitin' for you is all," Calhoun said quietly, eyes on the woman's.

"Hogvash," the woman snapped. "You don't know me from the bartender."

"True," Calhoun readily agreed. "But you're the best lookin' woman I've seen in here tonight. What's your name?"

"Gertrude. Most people call me Dutch Trude." She looked at Calhoun blandly, not taken in by his kind words. He was nothing more than another drifting hardcase with only one thing on his mind, as far as she was concerned. She would just as soon get it over with, collect her fee, and move on to the next one. She did have to admit, though, that he was almost handsome, and had a certain quality about him that piqued her interest just a bit.

"I'm Wade. You want a drink?"

Dutch Trude nodded and sat. She was glad to be off her feet, and she saw nothing wrong in sipping watered-down tea for which her customers paid whiskey prices.

Calhoun finally went upstairs with Dutch Trude, where he had a fast, nearly satisfying interlude with her on a creaking, squeaky bed much like the others he could hear up and down the hallway. Then he was back downstairs nursing another nickel beer.

A little annoyed, he watched Dutch Trude come down the stairs a few minutes later. It was not that he really cared for her; it was just that he would have liked her to show a little enthusiasm, even if it was faked. He finally shrugged and mostly put her out of his mind.

An hour passed, and then another. Still Calhoun sat there. He had nowhere else to go, and really, there was no place he'd rather be than in a lowly saloon like Hanney's. He was mostly content to just sit and watch the people around him.

One he kept a close eye on was a tall, hatchet-faced man with long, oily hair and flat, dead eyes. The man had swaggered in maybe twenty minutes earlier, and it seemed to Calhoun as if the entire atmosphere of Hanney's had changed as soon as he did. The man strutted and preened for a while, but few paid him too much attention. Calhoun figured most of the others were afraid of the man.

Calhoun noticed Dutch Trude coming down the stairs, and then spotted the man heading toward her. She reached the floor and was a few steps across it when she saw the man. She stopped, a look of worry, fear, and resignation covering her face.

The man grabbed Dutch Trude and started dragging her toward the stairs again. She fought a little, and the man smacked her. "Now, don't go actin' like that, bitch," the man growled. "I got needs and I been waitin' jist for you."

Calhoun waited only a moment, then shoved up and quietly stalked across the saloon. He knew he was being a fool, that he should mind his own business. But he couldn't just sit around and watch some insufferable beast manhandle a woman. It was, he had thought more than once, a failing of his.

Calhoun stomped up just as the man reached the stairs with his unwilling accomplice. Calhoun grabbed him by the shoulder, jerked him around, and popped him a shot in the nose.

The man didn't quite fall, managing to catch himself on the railing. He brought his other hand up to his nose, and it came away with blood. "Just what the hell's your problem, pal?" he asked, his face wrinkled in anger and wonder.

"You want a roll in the quilts with the lady here, ask her," Calhoun answered calmly. "She's willin', from what I figure."

"You know who the hell I am, pal?" the man demanded, letting some of his anger surface.

"Nope."

"I'm Sid Lockwood." He was surprised when Calhoun showed no sign of recognition. "I'm a power to be reckoned with in these parts, pal," he added.

"Don't mean shit to me."

"You're in deep trouble now, pal."

"That a fact?"

"Goddamn right." Lockwood launched a punch at Calhoun's face even as he continued speaking.

Calhoun sidestepped it and, as Lockwood stumbled past him, cracked Lockwood in the back of the head with an elbow. Lockwood fell on hands and knees. Calhoun spun, placed a boot on Lockwood's rump, and shoved. Lockwood slid forward onto his belly and face.

Calhoun moved back a step or so and watched Lockwood, after taking a glance around the room. No one else had moved, though two men who had entered the saloon shortly after Lockwood looked particularly interested in the proceedings.

Lockwood pushed himself up onto all fours, then rocked back onto his calves.

Calhoun eased out a Dragoon and cocked it, then aimed it at Lockwood's head.

Lockwood stopped moving, knowing what was going on behind him though he could not see it. "What now?" he asked.

"Stand and turn. Slowly."

As soon as Lockwood came around, Calhoun creased him in the center of the forehead with the barrel of his Dragoon. Lockwood crumpled. Calhoun then spun and fired the Dragoon. One of the two men who had looked interested in what was going on fell, a bullet in his chest. He jerked his finger and his own pistol fired, hitting the roof.

Calhoun looked at the second man. "You with these two?" Calhoun asked.

The man nodded.

"Come and drag this trash out of here, and then ride on."

The man walked stiffly up and bent to grab Lockwood. Calhoun stuck the muzzle of his Dragoon almost in the man's ear. "Ease your pistol out and drop it." When the man had done so, Calhoun said, "Now do the same with Lockwood's pistols." Finally he said, "All right, move on."

With a surly glance at Calhoun, the man helped a groaning Lockwood to his feet and out the door.

# CHAPTER

# 6

Calhoun was just finishing up his beer—and deciding if he should head to the livery to get some sleep—when Dutch Trude sashayed up to the table. She had disappeared just after Calhoun had taken care of Lockwood. Calhoun had wondered where she had gotten off to. He didn't expect anything from Dutch Trude, but he thought she might at least offer a word of thanks. Then he had shrugged and returned to his table. He had his own reasons for doing what he had done to help Dutch Trude; he was comfortable with that.

Now she came up to the table and sat. She gently set down a bottle of whiskey. "I vanted to say thank you for vhat you did, mister," Dutch Trude said.

"It was nothing."

"Oh, pshaw." She smiled, and it eased the hard look of her face a little. "Come on upstairs. I'll give you a roll on the house."

"You don't owe me nothin'," Calhoun said flatly.

"If I vant to give you one on the house, dot's my business," Dutch Trude said in a monotone. She was a little irritated, since she had figured he would be pleased with the offering.

Calhoun nodded. "Just as long as you don't think you have to."

"No," Dutch Trude responded seriously. "No, I vant to. Come on." She smiled again, and rose. "Ve got us a bottle and some time."

Calhoun stood. "What's your boss gonna say?" he asked.

Dutch Trude shrugged. "He don't haff much to say about it. There's nothink he can do to me."

Calhoun shrugged. "Then let's go."

Dutch Trude looked at him a moment. "Don't you ever smile, mister?" she asked.

"Nope."

Dutch Trude shook her head, either in sadness or sympathy; even she wasn't sure which. She grabbed the bottle, slipped her arm through Calhoun's, and they headed up the stairs.

"Roll me one of those," Dutch Trude said a little later.

Calhoun shrugged and rolled two cigarettes, then lit them both before passing one to Dutch Trude. The two smoked and sipped from the bottle of whiskey.

"Well," Calhoun said when he had finished his cigarette, "I best be movin' on."

"You haff a place to stay?" Dutch Trude heard

herself asking. That surprised her a little. She was not one of those moon-eyed young women in this profession who was just waiting to be swept off her feet by some gallant young man. Still, there was a certain amount of excitement in having Calhoun with her.

"I was just figurin' on sleepin' over at the livery. Get an early start tomorrow."

"Stay here," Dutch Trude said, shocking herself again. She mentally shrugged it off.

Calhoun looked at her, eyebrows raised in question.

Dutch Trude nodded. "Yah, I mean it."

"It ain't necessary."

"I know dot. I vant dis, too."

Calhoun nodded and plopped back down on the bed.

Dutch Trude rose. "You vait here. I'll be back in a minute." She grabbed a robe and pulled it around herself as she headed out the door.

A little puzzled, Calhoun leaned back and rolled another cigarette. He certainly didn't mind waiting a little for Dutch Trude to return. She was a mostly pleasing looking woman of about twenty-three. She was blonde, and had a squarish, broad face. Calhoun thought she was well built, being just a tad on the plump side as she was, though she was a bit top-heavy for his tastes. Her eyes were deep, crystal blue. And she had about the whitest flesh he had ever seen. It was almost eerie.

Calhoun heard Dutch Trude returning, and he reached over and casually pulled over one of his Dragoons. He thumbed back the hammer and rested the pistol on the bed at his side, his right hand still wrapped around it.

Dutch Trude came in carrying a tray that was precariously loaded with food. She was so interested in not spilling anything that she never saw Calhoun's pistol as he put it away once he was sure she was alone. Since there was no table in the room, she set the tray down on the foot of the bed. "I thought you might be hungry," she said.

Calhoun nodded, stubbed out his cigarette, and picked up a pickled egg. Dutch Trude tossed off her robe, then sat and joined Calhoun in eating.

While they munched, Calhoun asked, "Who was that ass I had the run-in with before?"

"You mean you really don't know?" Dutch Trude asked, surprised.

"Nope."

"His name's Sid Lockwood."

"So he said. He acted as if I was supposed to shit my pants at the mention of it."

"Most men would haff, I suppose. He's Royce Laird's right-hand man."

"Who's he?"

"Ach, mister, ain't you . . ." Dutch Trude paused and grinned crookedly. "I think maybe you're not from around these parts, yah?"

"Yah," Calhoun said in a lightly mocking tone.

"Royce Laird's the biggest outlaw in central Texas. He's a killer and a looter. Everybody's afraid of him and his gang of men."

Calhoun shook his head in some amazement. He figured that if Lockwood was any indication of the men this Royce Laird hired—and one of his top men to boot—Laird couldn't be all that fearsome. But all he said was, "I ain't."

"You should be. He's goink to be mighty mad vhen he hears vhat you did to Sid. And to dot von you killed."

Calhoun shrugged.

"He'll come back here vit' all his men lookink for you."

Calhoun shrugged again, unconcerned.

Dutch Trude's eyes snapped in anger. She set herself to berate Calhoun, but he suddenly popped a piece of cheese into her open mouth. "Hush," he said.

She smiled and then chewed. When she swallowed, she said, "It's your funeral."

"You in any danger from him?" Calhoun asked. He wasn't concerned for himself, but he would certainly not like it much if his actions were responsible for getting Dutch Trude killed or injured.

Dutch Trude shook her head.

"You expect he'll be back tonight?"

"Doubt it. If he vas dot close, he vould've come in to Hanney's vit' Sid and the others."

Calhoun nodded.

Dutch Trude picked up the theme again the next morning. As Calhoun was getting dressed, she said, "Since you're not from around these parts, I vould leave here if I vere you and go avay."

"Why?" Calhoun had almost forgotten about Lockwood and Laird.

"Royce vill come for you. I know he vill."

Calhoun shrugged.

"He'll kill you." She didn't know why she was so concerned about Calhoun, only that she was.

"I worried about every gun-totin' asshole, I'd have to live my life in a hole in the ground."

"But he's a mean von."

Calhoun stared into her deep blue eyes. "So'm I, ma'am," he said quietly, and Dutch Trude could do nothing but believe him.

"I know dot," she said, irritated with herself. "But you should at least stay avay from here—from Hanney's."

"I decide I want to come back to Hanney's, Trude, I will. And ain't no Sid Lockwood or no Royce Laird is gonna stop me." He winked at her. "Now stop your frettin'."

"You haven't listened to a vord I've said, haff you?" Dutch Trude asked with a rueful smile.

"Nope." He touched one of Dutch Trude's cheeks with a finger. "You just watch you don't get hurt."

"I'll be all right."

Calhoun nodded and left. He walked down the stairs and through the almost deserted saloon. Outside, he moved swiftly to Knowlton's, where he filled himself good on a fifty-cent breakfast of eggs, ham, flapjacks, and coffee.

Full, he strolled down to the livery, where, with the help of the owner, Tim McCallister, he harnessed the team to the wagon. Then he rode down to the general store. He began reading off Millie's list of supplies to the older man behind the counter.

"This sounds like a batch of supplies for Miz

Fuller," said Richard Bockmeister, the owner of the general store.

"It is." He stared evenly at Bockmeister, whose eyebrows were raised in question.

When he got no further response from Calhoun, Bockmeister said, "You don't look like a farmhand."

"I ain't."

"But then vhy're you . . ."

"You gonna fill the order or not?" Calhoun asked tartly.

Bockmeister stared at Calhoun for a moment, then nodded. He suddenly felt clammy. He had not liked looking into those cold eyes. He hurried to finish getting the requested items. When he did, he asked nervously, "Is dot all?"

"For this order. How much?"

"Eight dollars and forty cents."

Calhoun put the ten-dollar gold piece on the counter and then stuck the change back into his pocket. "Now, I'd like some cigarette fixings." When Bockmeister laid them on the counter, Calhoun pulled a silver dollar from another pocket and put that change in the same pocket. "Obliged," he said as he picked up the box with Millie's supplies and headed outside.

He set the box in the back of the wagon and then drove to the mill. They were busy there, so he loaded the sacks of fresh-milled flour into the wagon himself.

When Calhoun was done, mill owner Tanner looked over the bags, counting as he went. Then he nodded. "That's right, mister. Give my regards to Mister and Miz Fuller."

Calhoun nodded and climbed aboard the wagon. Minutes later he was on the outskirts of Pecan Grove, heading northwest at a slow, even pace.

It was well into the afternoon when he pulled up at the Fullers' farm. He and Fuller unloaded the flour into the root cellar. "How come you wanted so much flour?" Calhoun asked as they were working. "You and Miz Fuller can't have a need for this much."

"That's true enough."

"Then why?"

"Old Bockmeister's an honest man, as far as that goes. But he can only pay for goods what he can sell later for a little profit. I keep this flour here till January of so, and he'll pay me three times for it what he'll pay now, because he'll be able to sell it for three times more."

Calhoun nodded. It made a lot of sense. "Doesn't he hold that against you, though?"

"Nah," Fuller said as he tossed another bag down. "Like I said, Bockmeister's pretty honest. He knows I do this. And I ain't the only one. The rest of the folks in Pecan Grove know it, too. I think they sort of count on it."

"Why's that?"

"Hell, if all us farmers brought all our crops in right at harvest, Pecan Grove wouldn't have a thing to eat come Christmas. This way, they know they'll pay a little more in the winter, but they also know there'll be something there for 'em to eat."

That, too, sort of made sense to Calhoun. He and Fuller finished their work silently, then washed up and headed inside. Millie had the table set and was bringing food out. Fuller said grace and they all began eating hungrily.

"How was your 'spree,' Mister Calhoun?" Millie asked as they ate.

"Quite nice, ma'am."

"You eat at Knowlton's?"

"Yes'm. Twice." Suddenly he stood. "I almost forgot, Miz Fuller." He reached into his pocket and pulled out the change she was due from her shopping.

"Thank you, Mister Calhoun. Did anyone give you any trouble in Pecan Grove?"

"None to speak of. Mister Tanner and Mister Bockmeister looked at me a little suspicious, as if they didn't believe anything I told 'em. But other than that, no troubles."

"Did you get drunk?"

"Mother Fuller!" her husband thundered in shock. "That's no kind of thing to ask a man."

Millie smiled sweetly and nodded. "Yes, dear," she said quietly.

Calhoun almost grinned.

# CHAPTER

# * 7 *

It took two weeks for Calhoun to finish plowing Fuller's new field, and by the end of it he was in the mood for another venture into Pecan Grove. He was also a little worried. He had found that he was becoming entirely too comfortable on the Fullers' small farm. The Fullers were friendly, easy-going people, if a little too pious and straitlaced for him. Millie's cooking was the best he had had in a long time, and Fuller left him alone when he wanted to be alone.

The feeling of comfort made him uncomfortable. It was not something he had looked for, and he was certain he didn't want it. Especially not out here on a damn farm. He had not been able to bring himself to stick to farming when he was married; he would be damned if he would do it now for people he hardly knew.

Deep down, too, he was sure that the longer he

stayed on the Fullers' farm, the higher the chance of trouble arising because of him. And the Fullers had been far too kind to him for Calhoun to want them to be harmed because of him.

So he was determined this time to spend at least a few days in Pecan Grove and to look at what he might do there. He was sure there had to be something in the town that would get him enough money to buy a horse and enough supplies to move on. To where, he did not know, nor did he care. All he knew was that he needed to get back on the trail somewhere, be on the move, away from the cloying entrapment of growing friendship.

When Calhoun was getting ready to go, Fuller asked him to take along a wagonload of produce. "Sure, it'd be nice to hold everything till winter and sell it for more," Fuller explained when Calhoun had asked why, "but we need some things now. Besides, old Bockmeister'd get mighty upset—and rightfully so, I reckon—was we to do that. Such a thing wouldn't be fair."

Calhoun nodded, not caring one way or the other. At supper that night, he told them he'd be gone for maybe a week this time. "Unless you need me to get back straightaway for somethin'?" he added.

"No, no, not at all," Millie said with her usual good humor. While Calhoun and Fuller smoked—Calhoun a cigarette, Fuller a pipe—Millie went about clearing the table. On one of her trips back to the table, she stopped at Calhoun's side and held out a small, soft-leather pouch.

"What's this?" Calhoun asked. He was fairly certain the pouch contained money, and figured she wanted him to pick up more supplies while he was in Pecan Grove.

"Your pay," Millie said with another smile.

Calhoun took the pouch and looked inside. At a glance, he estimated it contained about fifty dollars. He held it back out toward Millie. "I can't take this, ma'am," he said. He needed a horse and supplies, it was true, and he was down to almost nothing after his last spree in Pecan Grove, but he knew the Fullers were not all that well off, and he felt bad about taking it.

"But you deserve it, Mister Calhoun," Millie said firmly. "You've done ever so much for us since you've been here."

Calhoun thought he detected a note of sadness in the old woman's voice. He realized she figured he was probably planning to leave here for good. "I'll be back, Miz Fuller," he said quietly. "I ain't leavin' here without tellin' you folks first. So, you take this back. You can put it to a lot better use than givin' it to a man like me."

"What's wrong with a man like you?" Millie asked evenly.

"Hell, ma'am, I'm like to go spend it on whiskey and fallen women or some such."

"Nothin' wrong with that," Millie said, surprising both Calhoun and Fuller. "You're a young man, not married. It ain't like you was a preacher or somethin'."

Calhoun shook his head in amazement, but continued to hold the pouch out. "The sentiments are nice, Miz Fuller, but I still can't take this from you and Mister Fuller."

"You can if I say you can. And I do," Millie said

adamantly. She turned and grabbed some more supper dishes and left.

Calhoun looked at Fuller, eyebrows raised.

"You heard her, son," Fuller said gruffly.

"You need this money, Jess?" Calhoun asked.

"No, sir," Fuller answered, looking back at Calhoun. "And I think you know me enough by now to know I'd tell you if we did."

"I still think you two're plumb foolish." But Calhoun stuck the pouch into a shirt pocket and stared at the old breastplate of Spanish armor hanging on a nearby wall, thinking how out of place it was in this pleasant farmhouse.

He left the next morning, a load of corn, carrots, pumpkins, and squash in the wagon bed, covered by a piece of canvas. He wore his slicker, since rain had looked imminent as he and Fuller had loaded the wagon.

Calhoun was an hour from the farm when the skies opened up. The rain pounded down, and the wind whipped and slashed at him. The mules were not happy with this development, and they became fractious and hard to handle. Calhoun cursed as he fought to keep the two animals moving along as they should. It got worse as they went along, since the hills soon became slick with wet grass or mud.

By the time he reached Pecan Grove, Calhoun was tired from all his efforts. Still, he stopped at Bockmeister's like he was supposed to. He tied the mules to hitching rails, hoping they would not spook at a thunderclap, and went inside.

It was peaceful inside the store after the roar of the storm, and he slapped his hat against his thigh, sending out a small spray of water. He walked to the counter and waited patiently until Bockmeister finished with another customer. Then he said, "I got a load of produce for you from the Fullers."

Bockmeister was surprised, not only to see Calhoun again, but also because he had come with goods from the Fullers. He would've sworn last time that he was going to ride off. "You mind helpink me unload?" he asked.

"Nope."

"Good. Drive around the back. I'll meet you there."

Calhoun nodded, slapped his hat on, and headed outside again. He drove to the back, where Bockmeister was waiting. It didn't take the two men long to unload the produce, some of which was in baskets. Afterward, Calhoun followed Bockmeister back inside. "Miz Fuller says you can either give the money to me to take back or hold it here for her till she can get into town."

"I think I'll hold it for her," Bockmeister said nervously but firmly. "If you don't mind."

Calhoun shrugged. "She also said that if she owes you anything, to take it out of what's due her."

"I'll check my books, but I don't think she's in my debt."

Calhoun nodded.

"By the way, how are the Fullers?" Bockmeister asked.

"Just fine." He nodded, almost as if to himself. "They're sure fine people, the Fullers. About the nicest I ever met." He walked out, not waiting for a response from Bockmeister.

Which was just as well, since Bockmeister was taken aback. He was still suspicious that Calhoun was a hardcase who was going to do something wrong to the Fullers, but his statement had been so obviously honest that Bockmeister was no longer sure of himself and his thoughts about Calhoun.

Calhoun drove the wagon to the livery and unhitched the team. He left the mules to be taken care of by McCallister. Then he went to Knowlton's, ate, bought a small bottle of whiskey, and got himself a room at Trumble's, Pecan Grove's only hotel. He had thought about staying at Hanney's and drinking there, and maybe even getting one of the girls for a spell, but he had decided he was too tired, and too irritated, from having had to deal with the mules in the storm. So he just went to the room in the hotel, where he smoked and drank quietly while he read the most recent edition of the *Bugle and Call*, the town's newspaper.

After eating the next morning, he headed for Bockmeister's, where he picked out a new shirt, a pair of pants, socks, boots, and even a hat. Finally he asked for some cigarette fixings.

"That'll be five dollars and twenty cents," Bockmeister said.

Calhoun pulled out the pouch and extracted a ten-dollar gold coin and handed it to Bockmeister.

The store owner took the coin and looked at Calhoun warily as Calhoun put the pouch away.

"Somethin' botherin' you?" Calhoun asked.

"Ah, no. No. Nothin'," Bockmeister said hastily. He got change and handed it back to Calhoun, then gave him the paper-wrapped package.

"Where can I get a shave and a bath?" Calhoun asked.

"Lawton's. Across from Hanney's saloon."

Calhoun nodded and walked out. He turned up the street and was soon at Lawton's. He had his hair trimmed and his stubble shaved off smooth, then had an almost hot bath. He dressed in his new clothes, but packaged up the old. He figured he could still use them for working, whether it was back on the Fullers' farm or somewhere here in Pecan Grove.

He walked slowly back to his hotel room and paid for several more nights. Then he dropped his old clothes off in his room. He strolled around Pecan Grove, looking at the buildings, seeing what kind of businesses were in town, and trying to get some idea of where he might find enough work to get himself a stake that would allow him to leave this area.

Calhoun was aware that most of the women who spotted him hurriedly crossed the wide, muddy street, dragging their children with them. He was also conscious of the looks some men gave him—looks of fear or nervousness, even hate. He was used to such things, and while he didn't necessarily like them, he did not worry about them either. There was little he could—or would—do to change the townspeople's minds.

A man stepped out of the town marshal's office. He wasn't paying much attention, since he was still talking to someone inside. As a result, he almost walked into Calhoun. "Well, sorry there, mister. I . . ." His face went ashen when he saw who it was.

"Marshal," Calhoun said politely.

Marshal Sam Packard recovered his senses quickly. "Just the man I wanted to see, Mister . . . ?"

"Calhoun. Wade Calhoun. What'd you want to see me about?"

"That little fracas over at Hanney's a couple weeks ago."

"What about it?"

"What happened?"

"Shit, Marshal, it's been two weeks and you don't know?"

"I know," Packard said defensively. "I want to hear it from you, though."

"Some asshole was manhandlin' one of the girls there. She didn't look happy about it, so I separated the two of them. He took a swing at me and so I stomped him a little. One of his friends thought he'd shoot me while I wasn't lookin', but I shot him first."

"That it?"

"Yep."

"Why didn't you wait around to tell me that?"

Calhoun looked at Packard in some amazement. "I was with Dutch Trude all night up in the saloon. The next mornin' I was in town a couple of hours. You can't tell me you didn't know that," Calhoun said flatly. "You ain't got the gumption to come up and ask me a question, Marshal, don't you go tryin' to make me out the wrong one."

Packard's face reddened with anger and shame. "I don't appreciate such talk," he said tightly. "But I'll let you get away with it this time, since I'm in a good humor. But I'm warnin' you, boy, don't you start no more trouble in Pecan Grove."

"I didn't start the other trouble," Calhoun said

evenly. He chose to ignore the threat since he knew he would have no trouble taking down Marshal Sam Packard. The lawman was about Calhoun's height, though stouter, and turning to flab with age and laziness. He presented little danger to Calhoun.

"Well then, Mister Calhoun, I'm warnin' you to stay out of trouble altogether."

"People keep out of my way, there won't be no trouble," Calhoun said reasonably.

"Just heed my words, boy."

"And if I don't?" Calhoun queried.

Packard gulped and blanched. "There'll be more trouble," he mumbled before stomping away.

Calhoun shook his head in wonder, and then continued his tour of Pecan Grove. He saw no place he would really consider working, even if they would have him. Which they wouldn't, he figured.

As he sat down to lunch, he pondered his options. They were few. The livery probably could use a hand, but it'd take him forever to build a stake that way, at least as long as it would working for the Fullers. There was a gunsmith in town, and he might be able to hire on there. That might be a little more lucrative, but still, he would be working for someone else, and he had never been very good at that. There were no army posts in the area that he knew of, so scouting was probably out of the question. He might be able to parlay the fifty-plus dollars he had left into a substantial sum at the gambling tables, but that was a risky proposition.

Of course, he could always steal a horse, but he

had never been the kind of man to do such a thing—except, that is, when times were so hard that they necessitated it.

He decided during lunch that he would give himself a few more days here in Pecan Grove before making a final decision.

# CHAPTER

# ★ 8 ★

Figuring it was a little too early for him to head for the saloon—at least for an extended stay there—he went back to his room and slept a little. When he awoke, he headed for Hanney's with a small sense of anticipation. He didn't know quite what to expect at the saloon, but there was a good chance that there would be excitement of some kind, whether it came from a fight with men looking for revenge against him or from a roll in the quilts with Dutch Trude.

The bartender looked at him a little warily, but Calhoun shrugged and took his bottle of whiskey with him. He wandered around a few minutes before settling in to play poker. An hour later, he spotted Dutch Trude. He picked up his twelve dollars and change in winnings and headed for her.

Dutch Trude looked really surprised to see him. Since he had not been around in two weeks or so, she figured he had taken her advice and moseyed on. She said as much.

Calhoun shrugged. "I told you I wasn't that kind of man."

"Reckon you ain't." She paused a moment. "You lookink for a roll?"

"Yep."

"You got to pay this time."

"I know."

"Giff Fred over there"—she pointed to the bartender—"a dollar and ve can go upstairs."

"How much for all night?" Calhoun asked.

"You haff a think for me?" Dutch Trude asked warily. All she needed was some gun-happy drifter taking a fancy to her.

"Nope."

"Ten dollars. Pay Fred."

"Even if we go somewhere else?"

"Somevhere else?" Dutch Trude asked, eyebrows raised in question.

"I got a room at the hotel. It's a hell of a lot more comfortable than that little room upstairs."

"Yah. Same price. You heard dot, Fred?"

The bartender nodded and held his hand out for the money.

"Hey, wait a minute, dammit," someone said from behind Calhoun. "It's my turn with her." A young man grabbed Calhoun by the shoulder and pulled him around.

Calhoun, not knowing who it was, did not hesitate. He just kept coming and slammed a forearm against the man's nose. The young man—a fairly good-sized fellow, Calhoun saw—stumbled back a step.

"Dammit, Frankie," Fred the bartender shouted. "Don't you go startin' no trouble."

"Keep out of this, Fred," Frankie Kitchell snapped. "I'm gonna teach this goddamn nobody a lesson." He jumped forward, swinging a meaty fist in a big arc.

Calhoun threw his left arm up and blocked the punch easily. Then he slammed two punches of his own into Kitchell's stomach.

Kitchell let out with a *whoosh* as his air fled, and he almost doubled over.

Calhoun grabbed him by the back of the neck, lifted his torso up a bit, advanced a step, then snapped Kitchell's head forward. Kitchell's forehead hit the edge of the bar with a resounding *thwack*, and he sank to the floor.

Calhoun looked at Dutch Trude. "I sometimes think you're more trouble than you're worth." He reached into his pocket to hand his money over to Fred.

Dutch Trude wondered just how truthful Calhoun was being. She wished she could tell if he was joking or not.

Calhoun looked at her again. "Can you arrange for some food to be brought up to the room?" he asked.

"Fred can do that, can't you, Fred?" Dutch Trude said with a nod.

"Sure," Fred said easily. "What do you want and what room're you in?"

"Chicken, cheese, a couple of apples, if you can get 'em," Calhoun said, taking over. "Maybe some hard eggs. An hour from now. Room Fifteen. I'll take a bottle of bourbon now, too." When Fred handed him a bottle, he turned his gaze back to Dutch Trude. "Shall we?" he asked.

Dutch Trude smiled a little, warming up to the idea. She was still a little afraid of him deciding he liked her too much, but for now she figured she ought to try and enjoy this a little. He had been good with her the last time; she had no reason to think it would be different tonight. Besides, it was a lot better than having to be with another dozen men, none of whom would be all that kindly to her.

Dutch Trude felt only a little odd walking across the street in her working outfit. It wasn't the first time she had been seen in public this way, though she was never comfortable with it. Still, it did give her a little bit of satisfaction to imagine how much she was annoying the straitlaced ladies of Pecan Grove.

Just after getting inside the room, Dutch Trude turned to Calhoun, and he soon learned that he was about to get his money's worth tonight, and then some. Dutch Trude was far more enthusiastic than she had been the last time. He reciprocated.

An hour later, there was a knock on the door. While Dutch Trude—as naked as the day she was born—went to answer it, Calhoun eased a pistol out and held it ready. One could never tell who was going to show up at the door.

It was only two delivery boys, who certainly got themselves an eyeful while they brought in several buckets of food and a large pot of coffee. After they left, Calhoun and Dutch Trude, both still nude, sat at the small table and ate and sipped coffee. Then they took some time to have a cigarette and more coffee, laced with a little whiskey this time, before heading back to the squeaky old bed again.

Dutch Trude was not up to offending the sensibilities of Pecan Grove's citizens the next morning, so Calhoun did not take her to Knowlton's restaurant as he had planned. Instead, he had old man Trumble have some breakfast delivered to the room. After eating, Calhoun and Dutch Trude had one last roll before heading out again to Hanney's.

Marshal Sam Packard was there, leaning against the bar and sipping a cup of coffee. And Fred the bartender was behind the bar again.

"Vhat're you still doink here, Fred?" Dutch Trude asked, surprised.

"That goddamn Smiley's sick again. The boss rousted me out of bed this morning. Jesus, all I got was about four hours' sleep." He smiled wearily.

"Vhat're you doink here, Marshal?" Dutch Trude asked.

"Waitin' to see Mister Calhoun," Packard answered, straightening.

"What about?" Calhoun asked.

"The trouble here last night. I warned you."

"And I told you I wouldn't start anything. That young punk was the one started it."

"That so?" Packard said skeptically.

"Yep."

"It's true, Sam," Fred said. "Frankie took exception to Mister Calhoun goin' off with Dutch Trude, grabbed him, and tried to hit him. Mister Calhoun cleaned his plow for him. That's all there was to it."

"That right, Dutch?" Packard asked. He did not like Dutch Trude, or any of her kind.

"Yah. Frankie thought he vas to go upstairs vit' me next."

Packard looked extremely annoyed. He hated Wade Calhoun, and was afraid of him, too. Because of his first feeling, he wanted to run Calhoun out of Pecan Grove; because of the second, he couldn't. Nor could he issue another warning, since it would sound—and be—hollow.

"Well, dammit," Packard finally said, "try to keep out of trouble."

Calhoun shrugged. "One thing, though, Marshal," he said. "Why'd you wait till now to talk to me about this?"

"Didn't know where you were."

"Then you're one hell of a lousy lawman. I was in my room at Trumble's. That should've been one of the first places you checked." Calhoun was sure Packard was afraid of him and that that was the real reason Packard hadn't come looking for him earlier. From the look on Packard's face now, he knew he was right.

Packard grunted. "I got a lot of duties, mister," he said lamely. He turned and clumped out.

"Fool," Fred muttered. Then he grinned. "How about an eye-opener, Mister Calhoun?"

"Wouldn't hurt." He downed the shot, said goodbye to Dutch Trude and Fred, and headed out.

Calhoun spent the next couple of days wandering through Pecan Grove. He gambled a little, winning more often than not; drank some; ate pretty well; sported with a few of the town's fallen angels, leaving Dutch Trude alone for the most part; and again looked into the possibility of a job here.

The following afternoon, he was sitting in Hanney's, by himself, sipping a beer. He spotted Packard coming in, followed by Frankie Kitchell and two other men he didn't know. Calhoun didn't think much of it at first. Then he noticed that the four men were heading toward him and spreading out. He dropped a hand to the butt of a pistol.

Seeing that, Packard whipped a sawed-off shotgun out from under his long coat. Another of the men did the same. Kitchell and the fourth man drew pistols.

"Go 'head, boy, pull that pistol," Packard said tightly. His voice held command now, as if he had found some backbone in the scattergun and the men backing him up.

Calhoun eased his hand away from his revolver and placed both hands flat on the table. "What's this all about, Marshal?" he asked quietly.

"As if you didn't know."

"If I knew, I wouldn't have asked."

"That goddamn innocent act won't wash here, boy," Packard growled. "Now stand up."

Calhoun could see no reason to ask more questions; it was obvious Packard was not going to tell him anything. So he stood, leaving his hands on the table.

"Ease out your pistols one at a time and push 'em across the table," Packard said, speaking as he moved a little closer to Calhoun. The shotgun never wavered.

Calhoun did as he was told. His bowie knife and

dagger followed. He took heart in figuring that the lawman did not know about his backup gun.

One of the men Calhoun didn't know picked up his weapons from the table and shoved them in his belt.

"All right, mister, now move," Packard ordered.

"You want to shoot me, Marshal, you don't have to do it in the back," Calhoun said flatly.

"I ain't gonna shoot you," Packard said edgily. "I aim to see that you stand trial and hang. All legal-like. Show you what kind of lawman I am, damn you."

"All this because of that dumb little bastard?" Calhoun asked, pointing to Kitchell.

"No," Packard snarled. "Now move."

Calhoun shrugged and walked around the table. He headed outside, knowing the four armed men were still behind him. He figured that Kitchell was just aching to shoot him. He also figured that Packard had spoken the truth. He just hoped Packard could keep Kitchell under control. He wasn't afraid of dying; never had been. But he wanted to find out what this was all about first.

Calhoun turned right outside the saloon and headed up the street. He ignored the looks he received now—looks of relief and superiority—with the same aplomb with which he had ignored the ones of fear and loathing before.

A few minutes later, he was firmly locked inside the Pecan Grove jail. It had only two cells, with a walkway in front that led to the marshal's office. There were three men in the other cell. Two looked as if they were sleeping off a drunk; the other just looked dejected.

Calhoun sat on the creaking wooden bed and rolled a cigarette. None of this made any sense to him. Packard might be a poor excuse for a lawman, but he seemed to have enough sense not to pull something like this just because of wounded pride. Calhoun also didn't figure Packard would do this just because he had beaten up on Frankie Kitchell. And he was fairly certain that even the combination of these two things would not have caused Packard to go this far.

Trouble was, Calhoun had no other possible explanation for why he had been arrested. Except for . . . "Hey, Marshal," Calhoun called, "this because of that feller I shot the last time I was in town?"

"No," Packard said from the office. Then he and his three men walked out, leaving Calhoun alone.

# CHAPTER

# *9*

"I'd like to pay Mister Calhoun's fine," Dutch Trude said to Marshal Sam Packard. "Or his bail, if that's what it takes." She had found out what happened only minutes after he had been arrested. She had put on her only decent dress right away and hurried over to the marshal's office, not quite sure why. She liked Calhoun enough—he was about the first man who had ever treated her decently—but there was more to it than that. She tried not to think about it too much, though, simply telling herself that he had been nice to her and that the least she could do in return was to pay what she expected would be a small fine or bail.

Sitting in his cell, Calhoun could hear.

"You can't do either, Dutch," Packard said stiffly.

"Vhy?"

"Because it ain't that easy."

"Vhat's this all about den?" Dutch Trude asked, a

sudden sense of dread invading her stomach. "All you arrested him for was beatink the snot out of Frankie the other day."

"It's far more serious than that," Packard allowed.

"Vhat vas he arrested for?"

"That's none of your concern, Dutch," Packard snapped.

"Marshal," Dutch Trude said, "I know your feelinks about me and the others who are like me. But I von't be treated like a child. Vhy has he been arrested?"

"Because I think he broke the law."

"By doink vhat?" Some exasperation had crept into Dutch Trude's voice.

Calhoun could hear Packard sigh heavily. It sounded exaggerated. "By killin' Mister and Miz Fuller," the lawman finally said after some moments' hesitation.

Calhoun felt an all-too-familiar pain in his gut when he heard the news from in the back of his cell.

"Dot's ridiculous." The words had just popped out of her, but once Dutch Trude gave them a moment's thought, she realized she believed them. She didn't know why, she was just absolutely certain that Calhoun would do no such thing.

"Is it?" Packard got up and paced a little. "No one knows where this drifter came from or what he was doin' out at the Fullers' place. When he come into town the last time, he had just a few dollars on him, as best anyone could tell. The first thing he does is beat the snot out of a man tryin' to do business with a common whore."

Dutch Trude bit back the retort she wanted to make.

"Then he goes and shoots down another innocent man."

Dutch Trude could no longer hold back. "Innocent?" she sputtered. "How can you say any man who rides vit' Royce Laird is innocent?"

"You don't know he rides with Laird or anyone else."

"Vell, ve know for certain that Sid Lockwood is von of Laird's men."

"Do we?" Packard said sarcastically. He was not about to admit to knowing any such thing. "I don't, but I expect you do."

"You son of a . . ."

"Watch your mouth, whore," Packard snapped. "Look at the facts. Your friend in there does those things. Then the other day he beats the hell out of poor Frankie Kitchell, an innocent boy, and again it's to protect a whore. Maybe it's this Mister Calhoun who's in with Royce Laird. It wouldn't be such a far-fetched idea. Not considerin' how close he's become to you—and what you've been to Laird."

Enraged, Dutch Trude spun and headed for the door. When she got there, she suddenly whirled back. "You ain't gettink avay vit' this so easy, Marshal," she snapped, voice ragged. "You think you can throw suspicion on me for somethink that happened days or veeks ago, and I'll forget vhy I come here. But I don't do that. Vhy do you think Mister Calhoun killed . . . these people, whatever you said their name vas?"

"Fuller. Jess and Millie Fuller. A couple of old

farmers half a day's ride or so northwest of here. Good people. God-fearin' people. Never hurt no one that I know of."

"So vhy voud Calhoun kill them?"

"Hell if I know."

Dutch Trude cursed silently at herself. Packard was not going to give her an inch, and she would have to ask exactly what she meant if she was going to get any information at all out of him. "So vhat makes you think he killed them?"

"Like I said, just the reputation he's got in the little time he's been in Pecan Grove."

"Dot's not enough."

The marshal shrugged. "Maybe not. But there's other things. He seemed to have almost no money the last time he was in town, but this time he had a whole pouch of gold coins. Old Bockmeister was suspicious of your Mister Calhoun right from the start. So was I, for that matter," he added defensively. "Somethin' didn't seem right to Bockmeister when Calhoun came in the store the other day with all that money. So he headed out there first thing this morning. He found the Fullers dead in their house. They were known to keep a tin of money stashed away for emergencies. That was gone. He raced back here and reported the murders to me. That's when we arrested Calhoun."

"But dot doesn't mean—"

"It should seem obvious even to you that Calhoun killed the Fullers, stole what little money they had saved, and then came here to have a spree."

"I heard he brought in a load of produce or somethink."

"He did."

"Vhy would he do dot if he had just killed those people?" Dutch Trude demanded. She was agitated. The evidence seemed overwhelming, though circumstantial, and she could think of no other way for it to have happened; yet she still was certain deep inside that Calhoun had not done it.

"To cover his tracks. He comes ridin' in here with that wagon of goods and nobody'd think anything was amiss back at the farm. He could have himself a fine old time here on those poor old folks' money. Then he could make out like he's goin' back there to help them some more, and disappear."

"Dot's as ridiculous as everythink else you've said," Dutch Trude said heatedly. "If he vanted to haff himself a spree or somethink, vhy come here? He could've rode off and no von would've known those people were dead for days or maybe even veeks."

"Maybe because he wanted to come back and see a certain whore," Packard said harshly. "One that was in cahoots with him, and maybe with Laird, too."

"You haff lost your reason, Marshal," Dutch Trude said.

"I'll lock you up, too, you disgustin' whore, if you say such a thing again. Now go back to your salacious activities and leave me to do my job in peace."

"I'd like to see Mister Calhoun."

"No. Now get out of my office before I throw you in a cell."

"You vill regret this, Marshal. Yah." Dutch Trude stomped out, anger and determination clouding her pudgily pretty face.

She returned to the office just after dark. Accompanying her was Cornelius Silver.

"We'd like to see Mister Calhoun," Silver said.

"No. Take your whore and get out of here," Packard snarled.

"I'm Mister Calhoun's attorney," Silver said evenly. "Now let me and the young lady go back there and see him."

"Or what?" Packard sneered.

"Or I will kick your ass so goddamn hard you'll be wearing it for a necklace." Silver might have been educated and all, but he was a big man who, unlike Packard, had not let himself become fat and sloppy. "Now, Pecan Grove being in the sovereign state of Texas, Mister Calhoun has the right to be defended against any and all accusations. I aim to do that."

"Son of a bitch," Packard muttered as he rose. Then he smirked. "I'll have to check you for weapons." The smirk grew. "Both of you."

"I'm unarmed, Marshal, and you damn well know it."

"I'll have to check anyway," Packard insisted.

"If you lay a hand on either me or the young lady, I'll pound your fat ass into the ground, and then I'll file a complaint against you with the county sheriff," Silver added pointedly.

Packard glared daggers at Silver. Then he shrugged. "Go on back," he said. "But I'm not lettin' you inside the cell with him."

Silver nodded. "Thank you. Now, if you'd please bring a chair back there for the lady." It was not a request.

"I'll be damned if I'll go cartin' around chairs for a common whore," Packard said, apoplectic.

"You're trying my patience, Sam," Silver said coldly. "Now do as I say." He turned and walked through the open doorway toward the small cell block. Dutch Trude followed him. Silver stopped in front of Calhoun's cell and waited. A moment later a grumbling Sam Packard arrived with a chair. He set it down and stomped out.

"Mister Calhoun," the lawyer said, "I'm Cornelius Silver, your attorney."

"I don't have much money to pay an attorney, Mister Silver," Calhoun said without embarrassment as they shook hands.

"We won't worry about that now, Mister Calhoun." Silver pulled some paper and a pencil from his leather case. "Now, Miss Trude here says you didn't kill the Fullers."

"No, sir. I didn't."

"Can you prove that?"

"Nope. Just say I didn't do it. Which is the truth."

"The marshal and some others think otherwise."

"I didn't figure the marshal was capable of thought," Calhoun said with no hint of a grin. Dutch Trude did smile, though. "You might not believe me, Mister Silver, but the Fullers were about the closest thing I had to family—or even friends—since I was a boy. I didn't kill 'em. And I'll tell you this, too," he added, staring hard at Silver, "I plan to find the bastards who did kill them, and make 'em pay."

"That might be a little difficult, Mister Calhoun. The marshal and most others in Pecan Grove seem to have you already convicted and sentenced to hang."

"There's ways," Calhoun said quietly.

"Well," Silver said with an easy smile, "until that point, let's see if I can help you. Now, can you tell me what happened?"

Calhoun shrugged, but said nothing for some time. He did not really want Silver's help. Nor anyone else's. He had been in such situations before and had always managed to get out of them. He figured he would do the same this time, too. After all, he still had his backup gun. On the other hand, he was facing some long odds, and there was no good in denying that. He thought that perhaps Silver could help him get out of here legally. That would be the best thing, since then he could track the Fullers' killers without having to worry about posses and such. He decided it was worth the gamble.

"I come to the Fullers' place a few days after my horse threw me," Calhoun finally said quietly. "I was on foot and near out of cash. I asked them if I could do some work for a meal or two. The time stretched on some once I come to like the Fullers a little."

"What happened when you came into town the other day?"

"Nothin' much. Me and Jess loaded the wagon, then I drove on in. It rained like hell and I had a hard time with the mules so when I got here I was beat. Me and Bockmeister unloaded the wagon, I took it and the team to the livery, I had supper, bought a bottle, and went to my room over at Trumble's."

"You saw no one hanging around the farm? Anyone

on the road to Pecan Grove? Anything suspicious?"

"Nope."

"Where'd you get the pouch of money Bockmeister said he saw you have?"

"Miz Fuller gave it to me."

"A heap of money for a couple weeks' work, Mister Calhoun," Silver said skeptically.

Calhoun nodded and rolled a cigarette. "I think she thought I was ridin' off for good, and she wanted to make sure I had a small stake. I told her I'd be back, but she insisted." Calhoun shrugged. "Hell, I even left my saddle there."

"Your saddle?" Silver asked, surprised.

"Big, fancy Mexican rig with silver inlays and such. Had two saddle pistols, my rifle, and a shotgun on there, plus my bedroll and my saddlebags, with all my personal effects. There ain't many, but there's a few I treasure."

"So you left your saddle there to show them you'd be back," Silver said with a shrug. "That doesn't say much."

"If I'd killed the Fullers and was intent on gettin' the hell away from here, would I have left a saddle that cost so much behind?"

"You've probably got it hidden somewhere," Packard said. He was standing in the doorway, leaning against the jamb.

"What makes you say that, Marshal?" Silver asked.

"Bockmeister didn't say nothin' about findin' no fancy saddle out at the Fullers' place," Packard said with a sneer.

"None of this looks very good, Mister Calhoun," Silver said, looking back at his client.

Calhoun shrugged. There was nothing he could do about that. He had told the truth and that was that.

"You know of anyone who might've wanted to kill those people?" Silver asked.

"Nope. They were about the nicest folks I've met in a dog's age."

Silver nodded sadly and looked down at the few notes he had made. "I don't know how much good I'm going to be able to do you, Mister Calhoun," he said with a sigh. "But I promise you I'll give it my best."

"Can't ask no more of a man than that," Calhoun said.

Silver put away his pencil and papers and closed his case. He stood. "Well, Mister Calhoun," he said, "don't do anything foolish. I can't help you at all if you do that."

Calhoun stared at Silver, not agreeing to or even acknowledging the advice. He would make no promises he was almost certain he would not be able to keep.

Silver could see in Calhoun's eyes what the prisoner was thinking, and he shook his head. He and Dutch Trude walked out, past a still-smirking Marshal Sam Packard.

# CHAPTER

# ★ 10 ★

Calhoun didn't see Dutch Trude for two more days. Nor did the lawyer visit. In that time, Packard frequently taunted him about that, trying to get some reaction out of Calhoun. The marshal more than half hoped that Calhoun would try something. Then he could shoot the saddle tramp down without a second thought and save everyone a lot of time and trouble. At the same time, he was scared half to death that Calhoun would do something. He was pretty certain that unless he had Calhoun under the muzzle of a cocked gun, he would be in trouble.

Calhoun didn't take the bait, though. He simply stoically endured the taunts, knowing what Packard was trying to do. He would wait until the time was right, then he would make his move. Packard would pay for his indiscretions, Calhoun would see to that.

It was dark again when Dutch Trude did show up.

Sitting in his cell, Calhoun heard the office door open, then Dutch Trude's voice. "Good evenink, Marshal." She sounded calm and polite.

"What do you want here, whore?" Packard growled.

"To apologize for my behavior the other night," Dutch Trude cooed. "And to maybe make it up to you in some vay, if I can."

Calhoun was puzzled by the sultry invitation in Dutch Trude's voice. Then he shrugged. She had to live in Pecan Grove, he didn't. If she had to make nice with the lawman to make her life easier here, who was he to take exception to it? Still, it did bother him a little.

"Well, now, that's mighty nice of you," Packard said magnanimously. He still did not like whores, but he could at least be polite when they were being so submissive. "Would you like a cup of coffee, Dutch?"

"Yes, please, Marshal."

Calhoun heard the coffeepot rattle on the stove. Then came a sharp *thwack* followed by a thud, as if someone had fallen to the floor. Curious, Calhoun kept an eye on the doorway and an ear cocked for sounds. He could hear Dutch Trude grunting a little, as if making some great effort to do something. Then came the jingle of a key ring.

Dutch Trude smiled weakly as she came through the doorway toward the cells. Calhoun was now the only one occupying either cell. She unlocked the door. "Come on," she said urgently. "You've got to get out of here."

Calhoun nodded and swept out of the cell. He

stalked swiftly to the office, where he grabbed an unconscious Packard by the shirt, dragged him back to the cell, and locked the lawman inside it. Then he went back to the office. He found his gunbelt and checked his pistols to make sure they were loaded and in working order. He also checked the leather pouch on the belt to make sure the two extra loaded cylinders for the Dragoons were there, plus a supply of caps and paper cartridges. He swung the belt around his middle and hooked it. Then he slid his bowie knife into the sheath that dangled under his left armpit and stuck the dagger into his boot.

While he worked, he asked, "What's Mister Silver gonna say about this?"

"He's all for the idea," Dutch Trude responded. She chewed on her lower lip, frightened. When Calhoun cocked his eyebrows at her, she added, "There's not a hell of a lot he can do in Pecan Grove to help you. The townspeople haff their minds dead set against you. In fact, the talk has been growink about a necktie party for you. Mister Silver figures it's best to get you out of here vhile ve still can."

"What about you?" Calhoun suddenly asked, giving Dutch Trude a sharp glance. "You won't be able to deny that you were the one knocked Packard on the head and helped me escape. Livin' here won't be easy after that."

Dutch Trude smiled weakly again. "I expect to be the first voman to hang in Texas."

"I can't let that happen."

"And just vhat can you do about dot?"

"Take you with me."

"You vill kidnap me?"

"Nope. Just ask you if you want to go with me."

"Vhy should I do dot?"

"Because you can't live here after helpin' me. And because I can get you to some other town someplace where you can make yourself a new life. Of course, I ain't gonna force you. You don't want to go, stay here and tough it out."

"I vant to go," she said quietly. "I vas hopink you vould say dot, but I didn't vant to bring it up. I vas goink to give you a reason to take me, though, if you hadn't thought of the idea yourself."

"What's that?" Calhoun asked as he finished with his weapons.

"I think I know who killed those people. And I can help you find them."

"Who?" Calhoun had a suspicion.

"Royce Laird and his men. He might not've been the one to do the actual killink, but I'd bet all mine money he vas the one dot gave approval for it to be done. And he vas probably there vhen it happened."

"What makes you think he's behind it?"

"Some young buck came into Hanney's today, got stinkink drunk, and vhen he and I were upstairs in the room, he started talkink about how he and Royce's men had killed a farmink couple."

"Drink'll do that to a man," Calhoun said flatly.

"Not only dot, but because of my . . . past vit' Royce, he thought he could speak freely. He vas braggink, I think."

Calhoun nodded. "You're gonna have to tell me about your past with Royce Laird someday."

Dutch Trude nodded distractedly. "Yah. Someday," she said vaguely. She sighed, then added, "As soon as I got rid of him, I went to see Mister Silver. Ve talked." She paused. "And ve decided to do this."

"Why you and not him?" He thought it odd that Dutch Trude, being so much smaller than Silver, would be the one to come here and try to knock out the marshal.

"I thought it'd be better if I did it. Marshal Packard doesn't like me anyvay. Plus I vanted to come vit' you. Mister Silver argued vit' me, but I vouldn't change mine mind."

Calhoun nodded. "Where's this feller now? The one who told you about Laird."

"Still at Hanney's, I think. Vhy?"

Calhoun ignored the question. "We better get going." He took Dutch Trude's arm and started hauling her toward the door. "You got any money?"

"A little. I brought it vit' me, thinkink ve might need it."

"Horses?"

"No."

Calhoun shrugged. He was not above stealing a horse or two if it was necessary, which it certainly appeared to be now. He stopped at the door and eased it open, checking to make sure no one was around. Then he and Dutch Trude slipped out into the lantern-lit night. They turned for the livery.

Calhoun was relieved to find no one at the stables. Since he was such a poor judge of horses, he didn't know which of the two dozen or so animals he should take.

Then Dutch Trude pointed to a powerful bay and a graceful looking pinto. "Marshal Packard's," she said, indicating the bay. "And Herr Bockmeister's."

Calhoun nodded. Taking those two particular horses seemed apropos to him. He found two saddles and began putting them on the animals while Dutch Trude kept a watch out at the door. When Calhoun was done, the two rode out and headed for Bockmeister's general store. They tied the horses out back of the store. Once again, Dutch Trude kept a lookout.

Calhoun broke into the store. Two lanterns were lit, providing a little light. He moved around swiftly, picking up those few things he figured they would need—two bedrolls, two slickers, paper cartridges, caps, jerky, coffee, a little sugar, flour, cornmeal, bacon, a sack of beans, a small skillet, a small coffeepot, two tin mugs, two tin plates, two forks and spoons, and cigarette fixings and matches. He put the food into one sack and the utensils into another, hanging one over his saddle horn and one over Dutch Trude's. He tied the slickers and bedrolls behind the saddles, and put the ammunition in the saddlebags he had found with the saddles. The cigarette fixings and matches went into pockets.

"Hurry," Dutch Trude said anxiously as Calhoun was finishing up his work.

"Quit your worryin'," Calhoun countered. "Go on inside and get yourself somethin' to wear, but don't take too long about it. And don't bother to put it on just yet." He had something in mind, and Dutch Trude's indecently abbreviated costume would help in that.

Within minutes, they were riding back streets and alleys, until they stopped in the alley next to

Hanney's saloon. "Go on inside and see if that feller's still there. If he is, get him out here."

"How?"

Calhoun gave Dutch Trude a slightly surprised look.

"Dot might take a few minutes if he's still drunk," Dutch Trude said with an embarrassed giggle.

Calhoun shrugged. "Don't matter."

"What about . . . the marshal?"

"Unless somebody's found Packard, we're safe yet. And I haven't heard any alarms, so I figure he ain't been found. It's only been fifteen minutes or so. Now, go on. I'll be right here."

"You sure?" Dutch Trude asked. She was suddenly terribly frightened, worried that he would leave her here. She had invested too much in helping him to be left behind at this point.

"Yes'm."

Dutch Trude nodded and dismounted. She slipped into the saloon.

Calhoun waited, sitting on the stolen horse. He wanted a smoke but did not want to give away his presence in the dark alley with a cigarette, so he just sat.

Before long, Dutch Trude came around the corner of the saloon. A staggeringly drunk young man was half hanging on to her. He was laughing loudly.

Calhoun slid off his horse as the two approached. Holding the reins in his left hand, he grabbed the young man by the throat with his right and squeezed. "Shut up," he hissed.

The man's eyes widened, and he tried to focus. "Who're you?" he asked when Calhoun had eased the pressure on his throat and grabbed a handful of his shirt instead. The words were heavily slurred.

"Who killed the Fullers?" Calhoun asked harshly.

"Who?" the man asked dumbly.

"What's your name?"

"Paulie. Paulie Goodrich."

"You told Trude you and some men who ride with Royce Laird killed an old couple, the Fullers. That right?"

"Huh?" Goodrich's legs were rubbery, and only Calhoun's grip on his shirt held him up.

"Shit," Calhoun muttered angrily. He looked at Dutch Trude. "This son of a bitch is useless."

Dutch Trude nodded.

"You got a horse, Paulie?" he asked, looking back to Goodrich.

"Sure. Big, ugly chestnut out front of the saloon." His voice trailed off.

"Go get the horse, Trude," Calhoun said quietly.

"Vhat're you gonna do?"

"Just get the horse."

Calhoun waited until Dutch Trude returned. Then he slammed the back of Goodrich's head against the saloon wall. Goodrich did not even groan; he just sagged against Calhoun's grip. Calhoun lifted Goodrich and threw him across the chestnut's saddle.

"Ve takink him vit' us?" Dutch Trude asked as Calhoun tied the unconscious Goodrich down.

"Yep."

"Vhy?"

"Once he sobers up, I'll encourage him to talk to us. I think I can get him to tell us a few things."

Dutch Trude looked at Calhoun's hard face and

shuddered. Paulie Goodrich was in for a bad time, she figured. Then she realized she didn't much care. If Goodrich had spoken the truth to her—and there was no reason to doubt it, since no one else had known about the murders—then he had taken part in the cold-blooded killing of two innocent people. Plus he was at least partly responsible for almost getting Calhoun lynched. No, she found she could work up no sympathy for Goodrich.

Dutch Trude mounted her pinto, riding astride. Calhoun handed her the reins to Goodrich's horse. "Think you can handle this?" Calhoun asked.

Dutch Trude nodded. She knew that Calhoun needed to keep his hands free, just in case someone spotted them.

Calhoun mounted his bay and turned the horse. They rode back down the alley along several side streets until they were finally past the last of Pecan Grove's buildings, then headed northwest.

Riding next to him, Dutch Trude asked, "Vhere're ve going?"

"To the Fullers'," Calhoun said flatly. "I want to see if I can pick up a trail or anything. Besides, a posse probably won't think I've gone back there."

# CHAPTER

# * 11 *

Calhoun kept a steely grip on his emotions as he rode down the lane between the trees to the Fullers' house. He could see little, since it was still the middle of the night, but there was something eerie in the air, something he did not want to let inside him.

Dutch Trude was strangely silent, too, as she rode. In the moonlight, Calhoun saw when he looked back that way, her face was a pale blob of fright.

They had stopped only once on the ride to the farm, and that was when Paulie Goodrich had roused from unconsciousness and began howling with indignity about his position across the saddle. Calhoun had ridden back and stopped alongside Goodrich's horse, grabbed a handful of the young man's hair, jerked his head up as far as it could go, and growled, "Keep squawkin', boy, and I'll pound you unconscious again."

"Who're you?" Goodrich asked. He was still drunk, and his head was fuzzy.

"Name's Wade Calhoun."

"Where're you takin' me?"

"You'll find out, boy. Now shut up."

Calhoun stopped at the house and began to dismount. Then he checked himself and pulled back into the saddle. He turned and rode to the barn, where he dismounted and opened the doors. Then they all rode inside.

"Vhy aren't ve goink to stay in the house there?" Dutch Trude asked.

Calhoun shrugged as he lit a lantern. "It just don't seem right is all." He didn't see any reason to give any more of an explanation. He pulled Goodrich off the horse and tied him securely to a post, with Goodrich in a sitting position. "You open your mouth and I'll gag you, boy," Calhoun warned.

Goodrich, blurry eyed and suddenly frightened, nodded.

While Calhoun began tending the horses, Dutch Trude spread some hay around for bedding for her and Calhoun. As she worked, she asked, "Vhat about eating?"

"You ever cook?" Calhoun countered.

"Not much."

Calhoun shrugged. "I'll start a fire in here when I'm done with this. I expect that between the two of us we ought to be able to make somethin' edible."

Dutch Trude nodded and got their bedrolls and spread them out. Then she picked up some firewood from the stack in a back corner of the barn. She cleared a space and chopped a small fire pit in the dirt floor, well away from the horses and fairly near the door. She picked up a wooden bucket, stumbled around in the darkness for a little until she found the pump, and filled the bucket with water.

Back in the barn, Dutch Trude set the pail next to the fire pit. Getting Calhoun's matches, she started a fire, using some old hay as tinder. She pounded up some coffee beans, put them in the coffeepot, added water, put the pot on the fire, and sat. She was tired, and she figured she had done her part for supper, or whatever meal this could be considered.

Calhoun finished with the horses and set bacon and beans to cooking. He drank a cup of coffee while waiting for the food to be finished. He and Dutch Trude ate silently. Calhoun ignored Goodrich's pleading eyes, but when she was finished, Dutch Trude asked, "Aren't you goink to give him any?" She pointed to Goodrich.

"Can't see any reason to."

"But vhy not?"

"Drunk as he is, he'd probably puke it up straight off," Calhoun said flatly. He figured that was a good enough reason for Dutch Trude, and meant he didn't have to give her the real reason—that Paulie Goodrich was going to be a dead man before too many more hours passed, and he could not see feeding a condemned man. Not when they had precious little food for their own use.

Dutch Trude nodded, accepting it.

After a cigarette and a final cup of coffee, Calhoun said, "I aim to get some sleep, Trude. I suggest you do the same." He headed for his bedroll.

Not sure what to think, Dutch Trude walked

toward hers. Calhoun had seemed so distant from her, and she wondered if he no longer wanted anything to do with her. She could not see that he was hurting inside because he considered himself the reason the Fullers had been killed.

That was an odd feeling for Calhoun. He had not been close to his family since he was a boy, and he had not been really close to anyone at all since Lizbeth and Lottie had been slain. To have become at least somewhat close to the Fullers, especially in so short a time, was highly unusual for him. Blaming himself for their murders, as he did for the murders of Lizbeth and Lottie, made it all the worse. Because of all that, he had no time or inclination to deal with Dutch Trude right now. He just wanted to sleep, to let the blankness of unconsciousness erase the sight of dead bodies from his vision.

Dutch Trude lay awake a little while listening to Calhoun's even breathing before she, too, fell asleep, troubled by nightmares and worries.

It was well past dawn when Calhoun awoke. He rose, noting that Dutch Trude and Goodrich were still sleeping. He built up the fire, put coffee on, started cooking more bacon and beans, then strolled outside to take care of personal business, as well as to take a look around. No one but them was in sight. He glanced toward the house, and found it didn't bother him as much as he thought it might. The sight of the two graves did, though.

He walked to the lonely markers under the single tree that spread big, leafy branches over one corner of the house—a tree that Jess Fuller had planted himself more than a quarter century ago. Calhoun had overheard Marshal Packard say that he'd sent a few men out the day after hearing about the murders. The men had buried the old couple. Looking down at the two wood markers and the still-high mounds of dirt, Calhoun felt odd again. He wasn't used to mourning people.

Then his feelings began to change. Rage welled up inside him, building until it threatened to overwhelm him. Only then did he bring it under control enough to where it would not rule him. It was enough, though, to keep him going, pushing him on to find out who had done this horrible thing.

He turned and went back to the barn. "Go on to the house, Trude," he said quietly but forcefully.

"Vhat for?" Dutch Trude asked, surprised.

"Because me and Paulie have some important business to discuss here."

"Vhat'm I supposed to do up in the house?" Dutch Trude suppressed a shudder at the thought of going into the house where the two old people had died.

"Look for some food or anything else we might be able to use on the trail. Just stay there till I come for you."

Dutch Trude looked at Calhoun, then nodded. She did not like what she had seen in his cold eyes, and she was not about to argue with him. Besides, she had no desire to see just how Calhoun planned to get information from Paulie Goodrich. She left and walked hurriedly to the house, pausing only a moment before squaring her shoulders and pushing the door open.

Calhoun went to the barn door and watched until Dutch Trude had gone inside, then turned back and walked over to Goodrich. He grabbed the front of the young man's shirt and hauled him up roughly. It was not an easy movement for Goodrich, since his hands were still tied behind him around the post. When Goodrich was standing, Calhoun tied a piece of rope around his neck and then to a nail in the post two feet over the young man's head. He pulled it tight, forcing Goodrich up onto tiptoes.

Calhoun stepped back a pace to survey his handiwork. He was satisfied. "Let me tell you straight off, boy, that I ain't got a lick of patience," he said quietly.

"So?" Goodrich countered. There was annoyance and worry in his eyes, but no fear yet.

"So," Calhoun said quietly, "I'm gonna ask you some questions. I don't want no shit for answers."

Goodrich was beginning to get scared now. "Supposin' I don't know the answers?" he asked nervously.

"Depends. If I think you're tellin' the truth, you'll be all right. I think you're lyin', then . . ." He shrugged.

Goodrich licked his lips, but said nothing for a while. Then he said, "Ask away."

"Who killed Mister and Miz Fuller?"

"Who?"

Calhoun slammed Goodrich in the forehead with the heel of his hand. Goodrich's head bounced off the post.

"The old couple?" Goodrich ventured. When Calhoun nodded, Goodrich said, "A bunch of us."

"Who's 'us'?"

"Just a bunch of fellers."

Calhoun broke two of Goodrich's ribs with one punch. Goodrich sagged and was brought up sharply by the rope around his neck. He gingerly pushed himself back up to his toes, wincing and biting his lip against the pain.

"Who?" Calhoun demanded.

"A bunch of boys I ride with," Goodrich hissed.

"Royce Laird's men?"

"Yeah."

"Was Laird along?"

"Nope."

"He knew about it, though, didn't he."

"Yeah. He gave his approval."

"Who led it?"

"Sid Lockwood. He was the one recruited me to join Royce's men."

Calhoun had a sinking feeling in the pit of his stomach. "Why'd Lockwood want to kill these people?" he asked, fairly certain he knew the truth. "They never did nothin' to hurt him or anyone else."

"He said it was to get back at someone who had done him some wrong. Someone who'd . . ." His eyes opened wide. "It was you, wasn't it. That's why you're so interested in this, ain't it," he suddenly asked, fear sprouting strongly now.

Calhoun nodded. "Now that you know my stake in this, maybe you understand why I ain't got patience. Them two old folks were . . . friends . . . and your killin' 'em does not please me."

"I didn't know, Mister . . . I didn't know," Goodrich wailed mournfully.

"Where's Lockwood now?" Calhoun asked coldly, unaffected by Goodrich's pleadings.

"I don't know."

Calhoun's punch broke a least two ribs on Goodrich's other side. "Where?"

"We split up after we . . . after . . . I headed for Pecan Grove, since it was the nearest place. I needed somethin' to drink—to try to wash away the feelin's I was left with after . . ." He stopped and spit, as if he still had a foul taste in his mouth. "We were supposed to meet in White's Corner, south of here."

"Who was with you here?"

"Lockwood." Goodrich paused to lick his lips. "Buck Stover, 'Fuss Connover, Turtle McCauley—he got that name 'cause he looks like a damn turtle—and a feller known as The Pole. He's a Polack or somethin', and can't nobody pronounce his name."

"That all?"

"That was here, yeah," Goodrich said with a pain-filled nod.

"Laird have other men with him?"

"Yeah. But there's only two with him, far's I know—Mike Ferguson and Denny Harbaugh."

"Where're they?"

"After the ones who were on this . . . job, got back together, we were supposed to meet the others in Luster, out west of here."

"You got anything else you'd like to unburden your soul of before you join the Fullers?" Calhoun asked icily.

"The Fullers? You mean you're gonna kill me?" Goodrich asked rather incredulously. "After I told you all I know?"

"Yep." There was no sympathy in Calhoun's voice.

"But I thought . . . you'd let me go if I talked to you."

"Don't know where you got that notion, boy," Calhoun said. "But you don't really think I'd let you ride away from here after what you done to the Fullers, do you?"

Goodrich sucked in a breath and grimaced as it hurt his several broken ribs. He blew the breath out and shook his head. He wouldn't let someone go under the circumstances either. "Nope, reckon not."

"Who did the actual killin'?" Calhoun asked tightly.

"Sid. He killed 'em both. The others took part in it, too, but I just kind of watched. I wasn't too fond of . . . you know . . . killin' a couple of old folks just like that, you know."

"You're a lyin' sack of shit, boy," Calhoun said icily. He stepped back, trying to think of a suitably horrible way for Goodrich to die. He decided, went to get a rope hanging over one of the walls of a stall, and tossed it over a beam extending out over the door of the barn. Then he brought Goodrich out. Calhoun tied the rope around Goodrich's back and chest, under his arms, and once again tied his hands behind his back. He sliced Goodrich's shirt off and then carved several slits in Goodrich's flesh, none deep enough to do much damage. He just wanted to draw a fair amount of blood.

Inside the barn, Calhoun found a piece of paper and a pencil. He wrote ONE OF THE FULLERS KILLERS and then got an old knife. Back outside, he stuck the small penknife through the paper and then plunged the blade into Goodrich's thigh. Finally he hauled Goodrich up into the air and tied him off there. He turned and headed back into the barn.

# CHAPTER

# ★ 12 ★

Calhoun saddled his and Dutch Trude's horses. Leading them and Goodrich's unsaddled horse, he walked to the house and stopped. He noticed a few spots where it looked as if someone had tried to set the house on fire. He wondered—but only a little—why the fire had not taken. Then he decided it didn't really matter much, if at all. He went inside.

"Vhat's all the noise?" Dutch Trude asked worriedly.

"You don't want to know," Calhoun said flatly. "You find anything we can use?"

Dutch Trude shuddered, but nodded. "Canned food, fresh vegetables, bacon, coffee—the usual."

Calhoun nodded. "Pack it up in some sacks or somethin'. We'll be takin' Paulie's horse. We can use it for a pack animal."

"Vhat're you goink to be doink?"

"Takin' a look around the house," Calhoun said, moving off. He suddenly stopped and turned back toward Dutch Trude. "You didn't take nothin' personal, did you?" he asked roughly.

"No," Dutch Trude said, insulted that he would think she would do such a thing.

"Good," Calhoun said without apology, then headed for the next room. He searched the house, growing more and more annoyed as he did. He knew there were some things missing, but he couldn't put his finger on what was gone. He was just absolutely certain that Lockwood and the others had stolen some personal possessions from the Fullers. He finally sighed, figuring he would puzzle it out sooner or later. None of it would make any difference in what he had to do anyway. It just might be easier to prove to others that Laird's men had done this crime. It could go a long way toward clearing his own name. That, however, was secondary to catching the culprits.

Calhoun went back to the kitchen and grabbed the sacks of food. He tied them onto Goodrich's horse. Back inside, he said, "You can change into somethin' a little better now, if you want."

Dutch Trude had considered doing that on her own, once she was inside the house, but she had no idea of what Calhoun was planning to do, so she had stayed in the skimpy pantaloon-and-chemise-type outfit she had worn on the job.

Dutch Trude could not figure out exactly what she felt for Wade Calhoun. She felt something for him, that much she knew. It was more than like, though she didn't think it was love. At least not yet. Such things frightened her more than did knowing what kind of man Calhoun was. She could not—would not—permit herself to love anyone. But it seemed that here she had little choice in the matter. Her feelings were getting the better of her.

Still, there was something almost comfortable in having a man she could sort of call her own, at least for now. He treated her well, despite his rough exterior and his penchant for violence and trouble. And he excited her as no man had ever done.

Dutch Trude suddenly wanted Calhoun. But Goodrich's angry bellowing outside cooled her passion just as quickly. She nodded.

Ten minutes later, they were mounting their horses outside the house. Dutch Trude was now attired in a dirt brown, plain, almost severe cotton dress. It had long sleeves and a high collar, with buttons that ran all the way down to the waist. In addition, she had on simple, plain shoes and a bonnet that almost matched her dress. Calhoun thought she looked perfectly innocent.

Calhoun led the way, heading around the back of the barn. That surprised Dutch Trude, but she figured there was something around the other side that Calhoun did not want her to see. She could hear Goodrich still hollering out there somewhere, and she was afraid to ask what Calhoun had done to the young outlaw.

"Vhere're ve headink?" Dutch Trude asked half a mile from the house. She had pulled up alongside Calhoun.

"Place called White's Corner. You know where it is?"

Dutch Trude shook her head.

"How many of Lockwood's men do you know?" Calhoun asked.

Dutch Trude shrugged. "I used to know most of them. But he gets new men sometimes. Like Paulie Goodrich. I didn't know him."

"How about Buck Stover? 'Fuss Connover? Turtle McCauley? The Pole? Mike Ferguson? Denny Harbaugh?"

Dutch Trude nodded at each one except McCauley.

"Good," Calhoun said flatly. "I don't know any of 'em, except Lockwood, so you can point 'em out for me." That annoyed him. He didn't like to be beholden to anyone; didn't want to have to rely on anyone other than himself. But there was not much he could do about it, so he accepted it. He didn't have to like it, though.

Sometime during the afternoon two days out, Calhoun pulled to a stop. "Is somethink wrong?" Dutch Trude asked as she halted beside him.

Calhoun pointed. He had spotted the small cloud of dust a while back.

Dutch Trude nodded.

"Stay here with the horses," Calhoun said, dismounting. He handed his reins to Dutch Trude and headed up a small hillock, crouching and then slinking the last several yards. Out in the distance, more than a mile away, he could see a group of horsemen. He couldn't tell who they were. He wasn't even sure they were white men. For all he knew, they were raiding Comanches. Or roving Mexican bandits. He wished he had a spyglass.

Still, he had to assume it was a posse out looking for him and Dutch Trude. Any group he saw would have to be regarded suspiciously, since even if it wasn't a posse it could still mean trouble if the two of them were caught out here by themselves.

He watched until the group was out of sight. The men had been riding in almost the opposite direction of where he was heading, so Calhoun figured he and Dutch Trude were safe. Finally he scrambled back down the hill and mounted up.

"A posse?" Dutch Trude asked, a little frightened.

Calhoun shrugged. "I couldn't tell, but they weren't headin' the same direction we are." They moved on again.

They reached White's Corner late the next morning. They left the horses at a livery stable to be tended, then went to a restaurant. White's Corner was a dismal little place, though there were half a dozen saloons and two whorehouses in it. Calhoun and Dutch Trude made the rounds of the saloons. Since she was still in her "chaste" outfit, they would simply stop at the door of a saloon and Dutch Trude would take as good a look around the inside as she could from that point. Both figured that if any of Laird's men were in White's Corner, at least one or two would be in a saloon, even if the others were occupied with prostitutes or some other business.

They had no luck, though along about the third saloon, Calhoun became aware that someone was following them. It took another ten minutes for him to pick out the man, who wore no badge or anything. Calhoun wondered what he wanted, and determined to find out.

Calhoun steered a surprised Dutch Trude into the next alley he found, down it to the back of a mercantile store, and then around the corner. He held a finger to his lips to keep Dutch Trude quiet. She nodded and stepped back.

Minutes later, Calhoun heard a shuffling in the alley. He tensed. As a man stepped past the corner of the building, Calhoun grabbed him with his left hand, then punched him hard in the stomach with his right. The man doubled over, making it easy for Calhoun to drag him around to the back of the building.

While he waited for the man's breathing to become more or less normal again, he looked the fellow over. He was an older man, maybe in his mid-fifties, with a ring of graying mouse brown hair surrounding a sizable bald spot. He had a nervous face with a scrawny mustache in the center, and eyes that blinked rapidly and often. Altogether, he had the look of a busybody about him.

When the man had regained his breath, Calhoun said, "You've shown a heap of interest in me and the lady, boy. Why?"

"It ain't usual for a man to take a woman around showin' her the inside of saloons," the man said stiffly.

"That's true," Calhoun agreed. "But if that's what we're doin', why should that be any of your concern?"

"The people of White's Corner're mighty suspicious of strangers, especially when they're actin' so strange."

"It's a good way to get yourself killed, boy," Calhoun growled.

The man blanched.

"What's your name?" Calhoun asked.

"Quincy Miles."

"Well, Mister Miles, did you ever think we might've been lookin' for somebody?" Calhoun said. He owed the man no explanation, but he hoped that giving one, whether it was truthful or not, would keep trouble from starting. And, with a posse on his trail and a gang of outlaws he wanted still roaming around out here somewhere, he did not want any more trouble than was necessary.

"That could be," Miles said agreeably. "Who was it you were lookin' for?"

"None of your business, boy."

"I might know him. I know most folks in White's Corner."

Calhoun knew he had a choice. He could kill this man here and now, and worry about getting out of trouble later, or he could push the story a little further in hopes of getting rid of the man. "Her pa. Otto Strauss," he finally said, making up a name. "Know him?"

"Never heard of him," Miles said, appearing a little befuddled. "You sure he's in White's Corner?"

"Nope. We heard he was down this way, and we've been checkin' every place we come to. We'll finish checkin' the other saloons now, if you don't mind."

"I don't mind, mister."

"I'd also suggest you mind your own goddamn business from here on out, too. A man sticks his nose in where it don't belong too often, he's gonna get it cut off. Catch my meanin'?"

Miles nodded and scurried off as soon as Calhoun released him.

Calhoun shook his head. "Goddamn fool," he muttered. Then he and Dutch Trude went back to checking out saloons. They had no more luck than before. Just on a hunch, when they were done, Calhoun said, "Let's check 'em all again."

Dutch Trude nodded glumly. She was tired of the riding and tired of walking and tired of chasing elusive outlaws.

They still found no one.

"Goodrich said that after they met up here, they were supposed to go on to another place called Luster to meet with Lockwood and the last of his men."

Dutch Trude's flagging interest revived a little. "Ve going to Luster?" she asked.

Calhoun nodded.

"Now?"

"Might's well. It ain't but a little past noon."

Dutch Trude considered suggesting they stay in White's Corner that night, to make use of a soft bed. Then she decided she did not have the energy for either the suggestion or the follow-through, if he accepted the invitation.

They got their horses at the livery and then rode up White's Corner's main street. Calhoun jerked his horse to a stop when he heard someone call, "Hey, Turtle." A tall, hard looking young man with the hooded eyes and sagging face of a turtle turned and waited for three other men to catch up to him. They stood talking a moment, then the three walked off, and the one called Turtle strolled in the opposite direction.

"You think that's . . . ?" Dutch Trude started.

"Can't be no one else. Here." Calhoun slipped off his horse and gave Dutch Trude the reins. "Stay here." He strode up behind the man who had been called Turtle and stuck the muzzle of a Dragoon in the man's back. "Stop," he ordered. When the man did, he asked, "Are you Turtle McCauley?"

"Who wants to know?" the man countered. He did not seem angry or afraid, nor even annoyed.

"Name's Wade Calhoun."

"Who the hell're you? I've never heard of you before," the man said smoothly, still unconcerned.

"Get your ass into the goddamn alley over there," Calhoun growled, jabbing the pistol muzzle into the man's back for emphasis.

The man shrugged and moved into the alley. His incredible slowness annoyed Calhoun more than a little. The man stopped about halfway down the alley, when he was told to, and turned to face Calhoun. He still seemed highly unconcerned.

# CHAPTER
# ★ 13 ★

"You Turtle McCauley?" Calhoun asked again.

"If I am?"

"Why ain't you headin' for Luster with Sid Lockwood and the others?"

"I don't expect that's any of your goddamn business." Since he and Calhoun were only a few feet apart, he could easily see the rage in Calhoun's eyes, and so he added, "I've got some business here in White's Corner to take care of with some family."

"Family?"

"My cousins."

"Those the three assholes you were just with?"

McCauley nodded, anger deepening his own hooded eyes. But he was even-voiced when he asked, "Just what do you want with me, mister?"

"Wanted to talk to you about the death of the Fullers."

"Those the old farts up on that farm?" McCauley asked with a shrug of unconcern. The Fullers meant nothing to him. They were enemies of Sid Lockwood, and so he had gone along to help dispatch them. It was as simple as that. "What're they to you?"

"Friends," Calhoun said.

McCauley shrugged again. "Hey, mister, I'm sorry. I was told they did somethin' to offend one of my pals, so we went up there to set things to right."

"Killin' a harmless old lady is settin' things to right?" Calhoun asked. He was seething.

"Well, we just couldn't . . ."

"Vade!" Dutch Trude screamed from out in the street. "Enemies comink!"

Calhoun shot McCauley in the face without a moment's hesitation. Then he crouched and whirled.

Three men were charging into the alley. They saw McCauley go down and began unlimbering their pistols.

Three shots by Calhoun later, all three of McCauley's cousins were down. Calhoun rose, slid the one Dragoon away, and pulled the other. He swiftly checked McCauley. The man was dead; had been almost from the instant of the bullet's impact. On the way out of the alley, Calhoun checked the three cousins. Two were dead, the third was hanging by a thread. Calhoun ran for the street.

Dutch Trude raced up with his horse and the packhorse in tow. Calhoun flung himself into the saddle and the two of them galloped out of town, a couple of gunshots ringing out behind them. Then they were out of White's Corner and racing northwest.

They rode as hard as they could for as long as

they dared. In the doing, Calhoun had the fleeting memory of what had happened the last time he had done this. Had it not been for that, he wouldn't be in this predicament now.

Finally Calhoun slowed them down, though they kept up a fair pace. Just before dark, he spotted a copse along a creek and they pulled in.

Dutch Trude felt bad about not being able to cook. It seemed unfair to her that Calhoun should have to do that, too, in addition to everything else. She figured she couldn't do much worse at it than Calhoun did. So she decided to take the cooking upon herself, as well as the associated duties. While Calhoun tended the overworked, overheated horses, Dutch Trude gathered wood, built a fire, and began cooking.

While they ate, Dutch Trude asked, "You remember that fool who vas followink us around Vhite's Corner?" When Calhoun nodded, Dutch Trude added, "Vell, he vas hangink around vhen you confronted that Turtle fellow, and I think he heard vhen you said your name to Turtle."

"So?" Calhoun shoveled another spoonful of bacon and beans into his mouth. He was hungry, and therefore willing to overlook the lackluster cooking. Not that he could do much better, but he was at least used to his own cooking, having had to eat it for so many years.

"So, as soon as you said that, he turned and took off runnink. I think I saw him ridink out of Vhite's Corner soon after, but things vere gettink busy in the alley, so I can't be sure."

"You think Packard and the posse had been in White's Corner?" Calhoun asked, certain it was so.

"Yah. They must've been on their vay back to Pecan Grove vhen you saw them—if that vas them you saw."

Calhoun nodded. "Makes sense. I expect our friend Mister Miles was headin' off to tell Marshal Packard. Probably figures he can get some of the reward."

"Yah."

Calhoun thought it over a minute, then shrugged and went back to eating. "We'll worry about Packard and his posse when—if—they catch up to us," he said, still eating.

As they had before, they skirted whatever farms and ranches they came to—until they saw smoke pouring from one of them.

"Ve better go down and check on them," Dutch Trude said as she and Calhoun watched the smoke curling into the sky.

"Why?"

Dutch Trude turned angry eyes on him. "How vould you feel if no one had gone out to the Fullers and buried them? Had left them out for the buzzards and coyotes?"

She was angrier than Calhoun had ever seen her, and her remarks were cutting. "What about the posse?" he countered.

"Marshal Packard hasn't found us in the two days since ve left Vhite's Corner," Dutch Trude said evenly. "I expect he won't find us in the next hour or so either."

Calhoun shrugged and headed down the hill toward the burning house. Outside, they found two bodies, a girl of about fifteen and a boy of about nine. Calhoun knew there were other bodies inside the house, but he was not about to deal with the inferno to retrieve them.

Calhoun buried the two children, steeling his mind to what had been done to the girl before she had died. The chore didn't take long, and then they were back on the trail, heading northwest, trying to find the town of Luster.

Early the next afternoon, Calhoun got the familiar feeling of an itch between his shoulder blades, and he figured someone was trailing them. He looked behind frequently, and finally spotted a small cloud of dust. He looked around, but there was no real place to hole up. Finally he picked one of the many small hills and rode behind it.

He climbed to the top and looked around. He had a sweeping vista for a long way. If it was the posse behind them—which he suspected—he could keep them at bay from this hill. The posse had no place to hide either, except a coulee, and that would keep him out of the range of their rifles as well as vice versa. They could overrun him, if they decided to charge on horseback across a wide front, but he didn't think the men in a posse from Pecan Grove, or from most any other town, would have the gumption to try such a thing.

He went down the hill and picketed the horses. Then he got a couple boxes of paper cartridges. "You ever load pistols before, Trude?" he asked.

Dutch Trude nodded, nervous but in control.

"Good. If that's the posse comin' at us, I'll need you to reload for me." He handed her the boxes of cartridges, plus the pistol he had taken from

Goodrich. He had brought Goodrich's rifle, too, but a quick look at it made him doubt the weapon's efficiency, and he decided he would not risk it. That created something of a problem, since he had no rifle to use. He would have to let any enemy get reasonably close before he opened fire. Otherwise, he'd only be wasting powder, ball, and caps. It should at least make things interesting, he figured.

Followed by Dutch Trude, Calhoun headed up the hill. Both lay prone near the top, Calhoun right on it, Dutch Trude a little below, so she would be protected. While they waited, Calhoun checked his two Colt Dragoons as well as Goodrich's pistol. Though he usually loaded only five of the six chambers on his revolvers, he now loaded the sixth on all three. With the pistols ready to go, he set them out in front of him on the dry, crinkly grass. Then they waited.

The wait was somewhat longer than he had expected, but finally a band of riders came into view. Once it did, it took only minutes for Calhoun to identify the riders as Marshal Sam Packard and the posse from Pecan Grove.

"That's them, ain't it?" Dutch Trude asked.

"Yep. Scared?"

"Yah."

"That's a good way to be. Just make sure you don't make no mistakes reloading, though."

"I von't."

When Calhoun estimated the riders were about sixty yards away, riding steadily toward them, and a little to the left to get around the hill, he emptied one Dragoon in their direction. Then he tossed the pistol back to Dutch Trude.

Three men and a horse had gone down, but Calhoun wasn't sure how badly any of them were hurt. The nine other pursuers pulled up in a hurry, turned, and raced off.

Calhoun emptied another Dragoon at them, knocking down another man and another horse. Both animals he had shot jerked and rolled, trying without success to get up. One of the men he had hit was crawling swiftly toward his surviving companions. Another was doing the same, but at a far slower pace, and Calhoun figured he was out of the fight for good.

The posse men had stopped about three hundred yards off and dismounted. A few fired at the hill, but their shots fell far short of Calhoun. With his two Dragoons reloaded, he once more waited.

About an hour later, Packard stood up behind a horse from his position way out across the rolling land. "I want to talk to you, Calhoun!" he bellowed.

"Go ahead!"

"Best you give yourself up."

"Go to hell."

"This yellin' is foolish, Calhoun. Let's talk like men."

"Come on up here, then," Calhoun shouted back.

"I ain't that damn foolish."

"You have my word I won't do anything to you—unless you try somethin' first."

"Your word don't mean a damn thing to me."

"I ain't ever lied to you, Marshal. Make your choice."

A few moments later, Packard mounted his horse and rode to the hill. At the bottom, he stopped and dismounted, then walked up the hill. When he was near the top, Calhoun said, "That's far enough. Sit." Packard did. "Speak your piece, Marshal," he added evenly.

"You're in one hell of a heap of trouble, boy," Packard said. He was grumpy and angry and worried and afraid. "Lord, but you've left yourself a trail of blood behind you."

"Only blood I've spilled so far," Calhoun said, "is that of two men who were involved in killin' the Fullers. And three cousins of one of 'em, who thought to interfere."

"Bullshit," Packard snapped. "We've come by at least three farms you've hit, slaughterin' the residents and makin' off with loot."

"First farmhouse we've stopped at since we were at the Fullers' is that one back down the trail just a little ways. I buried a girl and a boy."

"You lyin' son of a bitch!" Packard said vehemently, starting to rise. "Why, I ought to—"

"Just sit your fat ass down," Calhoun growled. When Packard had done so, Calhoun continued, "I've killed more than my fair share of men, Marshal. Most of 'em deserved it. A few of 'em didn't, I expect. But I ain't ever gone around killin' women, kids, and old folks." His anger was hot and real. "And I don't hold with no fat, stupid, shit-town marshal accusin' me of such."

"Insult me all you want, Mister Calhoun," Packard said stiffly. "Justice will win out sooner or later. Mark my words."

"Piss on you and your idea of justice. You want justice, you find Royce Laird and Sid Lockwood and the rest of their ilk. Then you'll have the killers of Mister and Miz Fuller."

"Give yourself up to me, Mister Calhoun," Packard said in persuasive tones. "I'll guarantee your safety back to Pecan Grove. And I'll guarantee it there, too. Let Judge McElroy sort this out. If you're innocent, he'll let you go."

"You must think I'm as dumb as you are, you fat, stupid son of a bitch," Calhoun snapped. "I wouldn't last a goddamn minute once I put my pistols down."

Packard's face colored with choler. "You'll regret this, goddammit," he snarled.

"I already regret havin' ever met you," Calhoun said evenly. "But I got a proposition for you. You go down there and take your men back to Pecan Grove. That way no more of 'em'll get killed."

"You're *loco,"* Packard sputtered.

"Maybe I am. But you've got several dead men down there now. You keep doggin' my trail and I'll kill each and every one of you."

"You won't do no such thing," Packard puffed. He looked around. "Where's the whore?" he suddenly asked. "You trade her off to someone for a couple boxes of paper cartridges or somethin'?" From where he was sitting below the crest of the hill, he could not see Dutch Trude on the other side of the mound.

"Yep," Calhoun lied. "Got more than a *couple* boxes of cartridges, though." He paused. "Now, if you've said your piece, best get your fat ass off my hill. If you got any goddamn brains at all, boy, you'll do what I said."

Packard stood and angrily stomped down the hill to his horse.

# CHAPTER

# * 14 *

Nothing much happened during the long, hot afternoon. A dry, brittle wind slapped at them, stinging them with its heat and uselessness. Every once in a while, one of the posse men would fire off a shot in Calhoun's direction. None hit anything but dirt well down the hill. Calhoun did not waste any ammunition with useless firing. About the only time he took a shot after the first couple of volleys was when a few men ran out to retrieve the bodies of their friends. Calhoun got another one that way, and after that, the posse men stayed put.

Just after dark, Calhoun and Dutch Trude slipped down the hill, mounted their horses, and rode off. They headed west rather than northwest, hoping to throw the posse off. They rode slowly but steadily, not stopping until just as dawn was cracking the sky.

An exhausted Dutch Trude set about making some food while Calhoun tended the horses. While they ate, Dutch Trude asked, "Vhy'd you tell Marshal Packard that you sold me?"

"He had his mind set on that idea. Besides, I figured it'd help us."

"How?"

"Well, if he's lookin' for a hardcase ridin' by himself and you and me pull into Luster or somewhere else, people won't look at us so suspiciously."

"I suppose that makes some sense," Dutch Trude conceded.

"Actually, it might help you more. If I do leave you in some town—like we talked about—Packard won't be lookin' for you. He'll—"

"You aren't leavink me anyvhere," Dutch Trude said vehemently.

Calhoun looked at her, a little surprised.

"I vill make sure those men are dead."

"Why?"

"It's none of your business."

"I think at this point it is. Now what's goin' on? I know you had somethin' going with Laird at one time. Is that it?"

"Yah."

"But why suddenly get so enraged now? You've been like this ever since we found . . ." Calhoun's eyes widened. "It's got somethin' to do with that girl we buried the other day, don't it?"

Dutch Trude nodded, hoping that her swinging cascade of hair would cover her suddenly red cheeks.

"I think you best tell me about it," Calhoun said

quietly. He rolled and lit two cigarettes, handing one to Dutch Trude.

"I vas about dot girl's age," Dutch Trude said in a flat, dead monotone. "Livink in east Texas vit' my family, not doink . . . vhat I do now. I met Royce Laird and thought he vas the most special man in the vorld. He vas an outlaw even then, but I didn't care. He vas tall and handsome. Very suave and most persuasive in his talk. He convinced me to giff myself to him. It vasn't hard for him to do, since I thought he loffed me as much as I loffed him. But he didn't. He had his vay vit' me dot time and a number of times after."

Dutch Trude could still clearly see the contempt in Laird's eyes, though seven, maybe eight years had passed. She had been desperate for his love, and willing to do whatever he suggested. Until he had decided that she should spread her favors around to the rest of the members of his outlaw gang. She had refused outright, her love for him tarnished.

Her refusal did not put Laird off. He simply began spreading word that Dutch Trude—known then simply as Gertrude—would give her favors to any man. All of a sudden men she did not know were showing up at her father's door, winking slyly and offering a handful of cash to have a roll in the hay with his daughter. Adolph Heissel was enraged and soon cast his daughter out. With nowhere to turn, Dutch Trude went to Laird, who took her in, with the proviso that she do as he told her, asking no questions. Dutch Trude did not see that she had any choice.

Within days she was the concubine for the small gang of outlaws. And soon after that, Laird was pimping for her, renting her out to anyone who had a free dollar or two.

Laird's criminal escapades had the law after him, though, and to get away from the pressure being brought to bear, he and what gang members of his were left headed west into central Texas. He brought Dutch Trude with him, seeing her both as a source of pleasure for him and his men and as a ready source of income. Though that income might be small, it could be relatively steady.

The group, sometimes bigger, sometimes smaller, depending on the needs of the moment, moved around a lot. When things got tight, Laird would sell Dutch Trude's services as a prostitute. When his criminal activity was profitable, she was relieved of that onerous duty, though she still had to service the men in the gang. That was something of a relief, since there generally were no more than half a dozen or so of Laird's men at any one time, unlike the legions she had to deal with otherwise.

Finally Laird had installed her in Hanney's saloon in Pecan Grove. For a while he had come around frequently, not only for her, but to collect money from Hanney himself. He had his fingers in a lot of pies by then, including protection and prostitution. Dutch Trude also was expected to service any of Laird's men who came into Pecan Grove. There generally was a code word that, when uttered by the man, would be understood by Dutch Trude to mean he got special treatment.

In the past year, though, Laird had visited Pecan

Grove and Hanney's far less frequently. Most often, he sent Sid Lockwood to collect what was owed him. Lockwood always made a point of stopping by to have a session with Dutch Trude. He was cruel and foul with her, thinking that part of his manhood lay in beating her and debasing her in the most vile ways. She knew enough not to complain to Laird, though. He and Lockwood went back a long way, and she knew she would only make things worse for herself by complaining of her treatment at Lockwood's hands.

Many was the time she hoped, even prayed, for someone to come along and save her from this repulsive life. No one ever did, though—until Wade Calhoun had walked into Hanney's saloon and knocked the starch out of Lockwood without breaking a sweat. Dutch Trude supposed now that that was one of the reasons she had wanted to help Calhoun all along; had taken such a strong liking to him. Deep down, she saw him as her savior. She knew that was, in many ways, foolish, but stranger things had happened. Still, without any actual encouragement from Calhoun, she was afraid to let him know how she felt. And as she told her story now, she left that part out.

"So you've decided for sure that this is the time to end it?" Calhoun asked when Dutch Trude had finished her tale.

Dutch Trude nodded, no longer embarrassed or shamed. What had happened had happened. She couldn't change the past, but she was beginning to think there might be a chance she could have some say about her future.

"Seeink that girl lyink there like dot just broke mine heart. I vould haff been happier to haff died so young vit'out haffink to go through all I did. But vhat makes it vorse is knowink that Royce—or at least his men—killed dot girl."

Calhoun nodded. "He'll pay, Trude," he said quietly.

"You'll keep me vit' you?" Dutch Trude asked a little nervously.

"Until they all pay, yep."

"Dot's all I ask." She wanted to ask for more, much more, but she wouldn't allow herself to do that. Calhoun might be her savior, but that didn't necessarily mean he was to be hers forever. If he could free her from the specter of Royce Laird and his men, and give her a new beginning somewhere she wasn't known, she would be happy enough. She could ask no more from him.

They turned to their bedrolls then, and slept away the better part of the day. When they woke, Calhoun decided that they might as well stay through the night and get back on the trail the next morning.

They went west again, riding half a day before turning north, hoping that would bring them to the town of Luster while helping them avoid the posse from Pecan Grove. They passed two more devastated farms. Dutch Trude wanted to bury the eight bodies they found at the two places, but each time Calhoun shook his head.

"It'd take too much time," he said, not very convincing even to himself. "Besides, I ain't about to spend the rest of my life cleanin' up after Royce Laird and his goddamn butchers."

"They deserve a decent burial, Vade," Dutch Trude said firmly. She would have it no other way.

Annoyed, Calhoun took the time to bury the corpses, five at one farm, three at the other.

Knowing how Calhoun felt about having to do such work, especially so much of it, Dutch Trude came to his bedroll that night and was especially solicitous of him. She figured he deserved some special treatment for all he had done for her.

He was a little less grouchy the next day when they pushed on. After less than half a day's ride, they spotted a town. Something—a hunch more than anything else—kept Calhoun from riding in. He stopped by a lone tree on a small rise and tied the horses off, then loosened the saddles and sat with his back against the tree trunk.

Dutch Trude took a chance and sat near him, snuggling as close as she dared. Calhoun didn't seem to mind.

Actually, Calhoun did mind, but there were other concerns at the moment. He was not about to try now to sort out his feelings for Dutch Trude. He felt something for her, that much he knew. How deep those feelings went was another story. He would delve into such things later, if he chose to.

Right now, though, he was trying to figure out what was stopping him from riding into Luster. Everything seemed normal enough, but still he waited.

Two hours later, he spotted a group of men riding out of Luster. He came close to smiling. It was the posse from Pecan Grove. He could tell that even from up here. He also gave thanks for his instincts, which had kept him alive all these years, occasionally to his regret.

Noticing that Dutch Trude had fallen asleep on his chest, he sighed, troubled by her obviously growing feelings for him. Still, he didn't mind sitting here like this—though that, too, bothered him a little. He planned to wait another hour or two before riding into Luster, wanting to make sure the posse had plenty of time to get out of the town and well down the trail.

He even dozed for a little while. He had learned years ago to take advantage of sleep whenever possible, since one could never be certain when one might have to go a couple of days without any at all. He finally roused himself, estimating by the sun's passage that two and a half hours had passed.

He gently woke Dutch Trude, rose, tightened the saddles on the horses, and rode with her down toward the town. Once again the first thing they did was to have the horses taken care of at a livery. There was a good chance they would need the animals again in a hurry. They went to a restaurant and filled up.

Afterward, they strolled up the street. Luster, Texas, was one of the most inappropriately named places Calhoun had ever been. It was a dingy little town, appearing worn and faded. People bustled about but seemed to have no real purpose. Only the saloons looked inviting to Calhoun, and he was loath to leave Dutch Trude outside alone. He also did not want to bring her into a saloon, unless it was to identify some of the outlaws.

So they just walked, wondering what to do. They

casually looked into saloons as they strolled, arm in arm, though not long enough or hard enough to attract attention, as they had in White's Corner.

Suddenly Dutch Trude gasped. She pointed over the batwing doors of a saloon identified as the Shining Pearl.

"You see them?" Calhoun asked.

Dutch Trude nodded. "Yah. They're all at that back table there, near the faro table."

Calhoun spotted Lockwood, the only one he knew, and nodded. "Who's who—besides Lockwood?"

"Royce is the von in the fancy outfit. The handsome devil vit' the whore in his lap." She shuddered, the feelings for Laird still strong within her. Trouble was, they were feelings of hate now. "The fellow vit' the big mustache that looks like it's growink all over his face is The Pole. He is very strong, very good in a fight close up. 'Fuss Connover is the von who also has a whore sittink vit' him. The von who looks like a dandy. But don't let his looks deceive you. He is very good vit' a gun or a knife."

"So'm I," Calhoun commented dryly.

"Yah, I know. But no von vill underestimate you. Many people haff underestimated 'Fuss Connover, and died as a result."

Calhoun nodded. He seldom underestimated a man, but it was better to know up front what one might expect.

"Buck Stover is the dirty lookink von. He is goot vit' a knife. He likes to use an Arkansas toothpick. Mike Ferguson is the von vit' the big red nose. He likes his vhiskey. Oh, yah. But don't let him fool you either. He can drink all day and still shoot straight."

Calhoun didn't think it necessary to tell Dutch Trude that he could do the same.

"And the last von is, of course, Denny Harbaugh. He and Mike and Sid haff been together since I've known them. Denny is a heartless bastard, and has no fear. Ever."

Calhoun nodded again. "It's near time to make these fellers pay for their sins," he said. "But first we got some other business to see to."

# CHAPTER

# * 15 *

Dutch Trude was a little confused as she walked swiftly down the street with Calhoun. They had finally found their quarry, and here they were walking away. "Vhere're ve goink?" she asked, puffing as she tried to keep pace with Calhoun.

"Get the horses ready," Calhoun said flatly.

That made sense to Dutch Trude. If they did confront Laird's gang, they probably would have to get out of Luster in a real hurry. She relaxed a little.

Twenty minutes later, they tied their horses to a hitching rail next to a big, gold-colored horse. "You stay out here, Trude," Calhoun said as he headed for the saloon doors.

"There's seven of them," Dutch Trude said in horror when she realized that Calhoun was planning to just go in there and attempt to gun Royce Laird and his men down.

Calhoun nodded.

"You'll get killed."

Calhoun shrugged. "I've been lookin' to die for years," he said flatly. "But don't go wagerin' that I'll be the one dyin' here today. I've faced worse odds before."

"Vait!" Dutch Trude insisted. When Calhoun stopped and looked back at her, she said, "Let's get some help somevhere."

"Who?" Calhoun countered. He was irritated by Dutch Trude's interruptions. He had made up his mind what to do, and he wanted to get on with the job.

"No von, I suppose," Dutch Trude said sadly, hanging her head. It was typical of her life, she figured. She was just getting to like Calhoun more than a little, had managed to put the desperateness of their situation out of her mind, and now he was walking toward his certain doom. She didn't know if she could handle the heartbreak. She wanted to harden her heart to it, as she had always done before, but she found to her dismay that she couldn't.

Calhoun shoved through the saloon's swinging doors. It was cool inside after the blast-furnace heat outside. The decor was typical, with a poorly constructed bar and back bar. A painting of a reclining nude hung in the center of the back bar. Tables were scattered around, most of them at least partly filled. The gambling tables were in operation. A pall of smoke hung just under the ceiling. A stairway led to a second floor, where there were several rooms running along the back and the left and right sides.

Calhoun tugged the back of his shirt out of his pants so he would have access to his backup gun. Then he eased out both Dragoons, holding them at arm's length down his legs. He strode purposefully toward the two side-by-side tables where Laird and his men sat drinking and having themselves a good time.

When Calhoun was maybe halfway across the saloon, Sid Lockwood spotted him. The outlaw's eyes widened, and he turned to Laird on his right and spoke urgently.

Word went around the table, and the outlaws suddenly began to move. Both prostitutes were shoved roughly off laps and onto the floor. Buck Stover and Denny Harbaugh went for their pistols, while the others headed for cover.

Calhoun fired once with each pistol. One shot took Harbaugh in the side of the chest, and knocked him back up against the wall. He fell and lay there. The other lead ball only clipped Stover's left arm, since he had dove for the cover of a table a heartbeat before Calhoun fired.

Stover and then someone else fired back as Calhoun kept walking. An innocent bystander, trying to get out of the way, was cut down by the fire. A prostitute screamed and everyone began trying to get out of the lines of fire, scrambling for the front and rear exits or trying to find some kind of cover.

Calhoun held off firing again, not wanting another bystander to be hit by mistake. That possibility did not seem to deter the outlaws, though, and Calhoun was finally forced to return fire. He hit The Pole, but only creased his shoulder. Calhoun could not see Laird and Lockwood, the two he wanted most.

Suddenly there was the heavy roar of a shotgun from behind him. Calhoun dropped to the floor and rolled, not knowing exactly what to expect. When he came to a stop, he heard, "All right, what the hell's going on here?"

As Calhoun rose, the bartender popped his head over the bar and pointed to him. "That son of a bitch started it, Marshal," the bartender said. "Just walked right on in here and began shootin' up the place."

"That right, mister?" the lawman asked.

"I reckon it is."

"I'm Johnny Buford, marshal of Luster, Texas, and I don't favor such shenanigans in my town. You got some reason for such a damn fool thing?"

"Yep." Calhoun looked Buford over. He was tall and rangy, with a long, drooping mustache under a hawklike nose. He had the look of a former Texas Ranger about him. He cradled a scattergun in his hands, pointing it generally toward Calhoun. He also carried a Colt sidearm in his belt.

"What's your name, boy?" Buford demanded. He was a hard man, and looked like he had little humor about him even at the best of times.

"Wade Calhoun," Calhoun said almost defiantly, experiencing just a bit of satisfaction when he saw the recognition in Buford's eyes.

"You're a wanted man, Calhoun," Buford said. "Marshal Packard of Pecan Grove was here not long ago lookin' for you."

Calhoun shrugged. He still held his Dragoons loosely in hand, pointed downward.

"I'm going to have to ask you to put your guns down and come along peaceably with me, Mister Calhoun." He didn't need to add the "or else."

"Afraid not, Marshal," Calhoun said calmly. "The only way that idiot Packard is gonna get me back to Pecan Grove is in a box."

"I can arrange that," Buford said easily. He had fought Comanches, outlaws, and Mexicans bandits. He was not afraid of one gunman, no matter how good that gunman might be. Or might think he was.

"You'll likely be joinin' me in hell, Marshal," Calhoun said flatly.

"I can take my chances." Buford paused. "Just what the hell were you tryin' to prove here anyway?"

"I was after Royce Laird and his men. Goddamn outlaws killed a couple friends of mine. A couple of good, decent folk." He didn't think his explanation would count for much with Buford, but he was surprised by Buford's response.

"Royce is my wife's first cousin, boy," Buford growled. "Him and his friends might've had some troubles in other parts of Texas, but they ain't done anything wrong in Luster or the vicinity." He glared at Calhoun.

Calhoun stared back. "So that's how it is," he said quietly.

"That's how it is, boy. Now how's about you set them pieces down and we go about our business peaceable-like."

"I think I . . ." He stopped when he saw someone who looked mighty familiar moving swiftly up behind the marshal.

The man suddenly popped the lawman on the back of the head with his pistol. Buford's eyes rolled up into his head and he went down in a crumpled heap. The familiar looking man pointed his pistol at Calhoun. "You're mine now, you son of a bitch," he snarled.

Recognition swept over Calhoun. "You're one of Jess and Millie Fullers' sons, ain't you?" he asked.

"How dare you use my parents' sainted name, you murderous son of a bitch," the man said, eyes snapping with rage. He began raising the pistol. He stopped when he felt the muzzle of a revolver touch his back.

"Hand your pistol back here, mister," Dutch Trude said tightly. She pressed Goodrich's old revolver to Fuller's back and held out her other hand. She took the pistol when it came back. Then she backed away, until her back was pressed against the wall next to the saloon door. "Ve best get a move on, Vade," she said.

"What about Laird and the others?"

"Gone. Those that didn't get out right avay did so vhen the lawman came in."

Calhoun nodded. He looked at Fuller. "What's your first name?" he asked.

"Jethro."

"All right, Jethro, turn and march outside. First sign of trouble you give me, I'll put a bullet in you."

"Like you did my parents?" Fuller said bitterly.

"I didn't kill your parents," Calhoun said roughly. "They were my friends. That's why you're goin' with me. Now move."

Calhoun followed Fuller toward the door, trusting

in Dutch Trude to keep an eye on the rest of the saloon's patrons. When the two men were outside, Dutch Trude slipped out, too.

"Where's your horse, Jethro?" Calhoun asked.

Fuller pointed to the golden animal next to Calhoun's bay.

"Get on it."

"I ain't goin' nowhere with . . ."

Calhoun slapped Fuller on the side of the head with a pistol barrel, dazing him some. "Get on the goddamn horse, boy," he snapped.

Then the three of them were galloping out of town, racing northwest. A couple hours later, they came to a stream. They slowed the horses and entered the thin creek, riding upstream, roughly north.

A little more than a mile on, Calhoun told Dutch Trude, who was in the lead, to move out of the creek and head northwest again, toward the flats. Fuller rode in the center, with Calhoun bringing up the rear so he could keep an eye on him, as well as watch for signs of pursuit.

They rode until just after dark, when Calhoun stopped them. He had found another thin ribbon of creek and followed it a little, until coming to a section that had thick vegetation along the bank.

Calhoun did not apologize when he tied Fuller to a tree. Then he went to tend the horses, while Dutch Trude began gathering firewood.

Calhoun untied Fuller to eat. "Don't pull no shit," he warned. "We all could use a peaceable supper."

Fuller nodded tightly. He'd decided he would act civilized for as long as it took to get free and kill

Wade Calhoun. He sat and accepted a tin plate of salt beef stew with biscuits from Dutch Trude. He grimaced at the first taste of it. His wife was an excellent cook, and so he was used to eating well. This concoction was as foul as anything he had ever tasted. Still, he plowed his way through it, knowing he would need the food for strength.

After eating, Calhoun leaned back against a log and rolled a cigarette for him and one for Dutch Trude. Fuller looked reprovingly at Dutch Trude when she fired hers up with a twig from the fire.

"Somethink wrong?" Dutch Trude asked with mock innocence.

"Only women I know who smoke, besides Mexicans, are fallen women," Fuller said stiffly.

"You always insult your hosts, Mister Fuller?" Calhoun asked flatly.

"You're not my hosts," Fuller growled. "You're kidnappers is what you are."

Calhoun shrugged. "Perhaps," he allowed. He paused, staring at Fuller. Jethro Fuller looked like a considerably younger copy of his father. He was big and burly with a reddish, expressive face. Calhoun suspected that normally Jethro was a friendly sort of man.

"And," Fuller went on, as if he had not really heard Calhoun, "if you're goin' to kill me, you might as well get it over with. I ain't goin' to cooperate with you no more. So kill me and be done with it."

"I don't want to kill you," Calhoun said honestly. "I told you before, all I want to do is tell you what really happened to your parents."

"You can talk till you're blue in the face, mister,"

Fuller said defiantly, "but you ain't goin' to convince me you didn't kill my folks."

"How'd you hear I was the one who done it?" Calhoun asked.

"I knew about you—that you were at the farm," Fuller said. "May I have more coffee?" He filled his cup after Calhoun nodded. "Ma had wrote me to tell me about you. She never did say you were a gunman, though," Fuller added sourly. "She sounded quite happy to have you around."

"If her sons and daughters had stuck nearby, she wouldn't have had to take in a drifter," Calhoun said quietly.

Anger flared anew in Fuller's eyes. "A man's got to make his own way in life," he said lamely. After a couple of sips of coffee, he continued. "Somebody from Pecan Grove brought word that Ma and Pa had been killed and that the drifter who had been stayin' with them had been the one who done it. I wanted to come and get you, but I didn't know what you looked like or anything. Besides, Jane—she's my wife—didn't want me goin' off and leaving her and the kids. Still, the more I thought about it, the more it ate at me. Finally I left, and headed to Luster, figuring to go to Pecan Grove and see about trackin' you down from there. I got lucky when I found the posse from Pecan Grove there. I talked to Marshal Packard, but decided I'd go on my own. I was just finishin' up a beer when you walked into the Shinin' Pearl and started shootin' up the place."

"Very fortunate," Calhoun said sarcastically.

Fuller ignored the crack. "I thought I'd lost my chance to kill you myself when Marshal Buford came in and got the drop on you. But, well, things almost worked out, until that strumpet of yours interfered."

"Watch your mouth, boy," Calhoun said harshly.

Fuller shrugged. He figured he couldn't get any more dead than he expected to get soon anyway. He might as well make his views known while he still could.

# CHAPTER 16

"I don't expect you to believe me, Mister Fuller," Calhoun said quietly, "but I ain't the one killed your folks. Your ma and pa were the nearest thing to a friend or family I've had since I can remember."

"No, Mister Calhoun," Fuller said harshly, "I don't believe you. Not for a minute. Look at you. It's obvious to anyone who spots you that you're a saddle tramp and a killer."

"I'm both," Calhoun agreed with a sad nod. "But not like you might think. I've killed my share of men. Hell, I've killed enough men to last several lifetimes. Maybe some of 'em even didn't deserve it, but each and every one of 'em had tried to kill me or had betrayed me in some way."

"Well, I'm sorry, Mister Calhoun, but I'm afraid I can't work up a whole lot of sympathy for you."

Calhoun shrugged. "I don't expect you to. I just

wanted you to know that I know what I am, and I ain't what you think. I've done many an evil thing, but I ain't ever took to killin' women, kids, or old folks. I told you that before."

"Horseshit," Fuller growled. He was not usually a violent man, but his parents' murders had changed him somewhat. Although he was not a gunman, he was fully ready to kill the one who had slain his parents. The rage helped him keep down his fear, too. He would never normally give a well-established killer like Wade Calhoun such a hard time, but right now he was more interested in revenge than in politeness or fear.

Calhoun sighed. He could understand Fuller's feelings. To anyone other than himself, he knew, it must seem that he was the killer of the two old people. He wanted to prove to Fuller that he wasn't, but he was beginning to think that might be impossible. And if that proved to be the case, he was going to have to end up killing Fuller. It would be, he figured, an ironic testament to his wretched life to end up killing the son of two people he was accused of murdering but had not—two people whose murders he had sworn to avenge.

"Would you like to know who really killed your folks?" Calhoun asked softly, deciding he had to make at least one more try.

"I know who done it," Fuller said adamantly.

Calhoun sighed again, annoyed, angry, dejected by all that had happened in the past week or so. "Whether you want to hear it or not, I'm gonna tell you," he insisted. "It was Sid Lockwood and several of the others who ride with Royce Laird."

Fuller didn't look interested.

"Those were the men I was tryin' to gun down in the Shinin' Pearl. I've been trackin' 'em since I got away from that idiot Packard."

"Horseshit," Fuller reiterated. "I heard Marshal Buford back in Luster tell you that that feller Laird was his wife's cousin."

"That means he can't be an outlaw and a killer?" Calhoun countered.

"Seems mighty unlikely."

"You're a bigger goddamn fool than I thought," Calhoun snapped.

Fuller glared but said nothing about the comment. He did ask, though, "Why would they—even if they were outlaws—why would they want to kill my folks? Ma and Pa never hurt nobody." He seemed suddenly dazed, as the reality of his parents' deaths had just hit him again.

"Because," Calhoun said flatly, "I kicked the shit out of Lockwood back in Pecan Grove. He was afraid to come against me. He learned that I had been stayin' with your folks, so he killed them, knowin' I'd be blamed for it and most likely hang. Hell of a way to get revenge."

Fuller's certainty of Calhoun being the killer was suddenly shaken. He still thought he was the murderer, but he was no longer quite as positive. What he had said had the sound of truth to it. Still, Fuller had to believe that Calhoun was the killer. "That's an unlikely sounding tale, Mister Calhoun," he said quietly.

"It is?" Dutch Trude interjected.

"Yes'm. Sounds contrived to me."

"Answer me this then," Calhoun said. "If I was

plannin' to kill your folks, why would I have spent more than two weeks helpin' Jess plow a new field? That ain't easy work, nor work that I'm fond of."

"Maybe you were waitin' to find out where they kept their small can of savin's."

"You don't think I could've gotten that information out of 'em, if I was plannin' to kill 'em anyway?" Calhoun demanded, eyes snapping. He was sick and tired of tracking Laird's men; and he was disgusted with wasting his time in trying to explain things to Jethro Fuller.

Fuller felt a cold spot spreading out from the center of his stomach. Now that he thought about it, he could easily believe that Calhoun would torture his folks to learn where their money was. Trouble was, that posed a dilemma for him. He knew for certain that Calhoun was capable of such cruelty and viciousness, which would lead one to think that he was the killer. On the other hand, since he was that cruel, why would he waste a couple of weeks helping out the old couple, doing backbreaking labor no less, for a few paltry dollars? That made no sense. Fuller was confused now, and didn't know what to say. He still believed—or maybe he just wanted to believe—that Calhoun had killed his parents, but all certainty about that was gone. Now it was just stubbornness.

Calhoun shook his head, seeing the doubt and confusion in Fuller's eyes. "Maybe one day you'll see the truth of it, Mister Fuller," he said. He certainly wasn't about to explain it any further.

"I think I know the truth of it already, Mister Calhoun," Fuller insisted obstinately. "So do with me what you will."

"Shit," Calhoun muttered. He was of a vile enough humor to want to kill Fuller just for being so mulish, but he forced himself to calm down. "What I'm gonna do is take you with us," he said.

Both Fuller and Dutch Trude looked at Calhoun in shock and surprise.

Calhoun's lips twitched. "Trude and me're chasin' Laird's men. I still aim to catch 'em and make 'em pay for killin' your folks. I'm gonna drag you along so that you will see the truth of it."

"I'll kill you the first chance I get," Fuller threatened.

Calhoun nodded, understanding. "That's why you ain't gettin' your pistol back. It's also why you're going to be tied up every night. I'll have my eye on you all the time, Jethro. Anytime you think you can best me, you come ahead and try."

"You got to sleep sometime."

"I sleep lightly." Calhoun tossed out the last of his coffee. "And speakin' of sleep, it's about time we all got some. Trude, would you get Mister Fuller's bedroll and spread it out over by yon tree." He pointed.

When Dutch Trude had done so, Calhoun looked at Fuller. "Up," he said.

Still angry, Fuller stood, and then charged Calhoun. The saddle tramp partly turned, so that Fuller caught the point of Calhoun's shoulder in the chest. Fuller was so bulky, though, that he ended up spinning Calhoun completely around. As Fuller stopped and turned back to make another charge, Calhoun punched him hard in the stomach.

Fuller doubled over. Calhoun grabbed him by the hair and pulled his head up, then popped him a short shot in the nose. The cartilage didn't break, though blood began seeping out of the nostrils.

"Now, get over by the tree," Calhoun said.

Fuller glumly headed toward the tree and sat on his bedroll. After Calhoun tied him to the tree, Fuller stretched out. Dutch Trude strolled over to him and knelt at his side. "What do you want?" he demanded.

"I expect you don't like me very much, Mister Fuller," Dutch Trude said, "but I vill tell you somethink anyvay. If Vade vanted to kill you, you'd be dead already. He's had several chances to kill you, includink just now. But he didn't. Belieff him vhat he says to you."

"Why should I take the word of a strumpet?" Fuller demanded.

"Vhy do you say I am such a voman?" Dutch Trude countered. She was dressed demurely enough that one should not have been able to tell just from looking at her what she had been doing for her livelihood.

"Any woman who'd run with a man like that son of a bitch over there's got to be either a complete fool or a whore," Fuller said flatly.

"I haff been both," Dutch Trude admitted. "But beink vit' Vade is the right thing for me. I might be a fool again one day, but I von't be a whore no longer." She pushed up to her feet. "You should vait to see vhat people are really like instead of makink up your mind before you know all the facts, Mister Fuller. Just because a man looks like a hardcase doesn't mean he's an evil man. Some men, vons who look like upstandink men, can be outlaws and killers, too." She clamped off whatever else she had been figuring to say. *"Gut nacht,* Mister Fuller."

Dutch Trude walked straight to Calhoun's bedroll and lay down on top of him, ignoring the guns that dug into her hipbones. She kissed him hard.

"You sure you want this?" Calhoun asked when their lips had parted.

"Yah."

"What'll poor Mister Fuller think?" Calhoun said. "Won't he get the wrong impression of you?"

"He knows vhat I am—vhat I *vas.*"

"He one of your old customers?" Calhoun asked a little sullenly.

"No. He figured it out. He's not a fool, you know."

"He sure acts like it."

Dutch Trude rolled off Calhoun and onto her back next to him. "Take off your guns," she ordered. As Calhoun did so, Dutch Trude continued. "He's no fool. No, not at all. It's just that in this von area—about his folks beink killed—he is blind. He can't see or hear anythink other than vhat he vants to see or hear about it."

Calhoun could understand that. "His bein' blind about it's gonna get him killed, he keeps it up."

"Ve are all obsessed with things sometimes. You are now."

"Damn right I am," Calhoun said gruffly as he pulled Dutch Trude atop him again.

"Dot's not vhat I mean, and you know it," she said seriously. She rested her round chin on her hands on the upper part of his chest, so she could look at him. "You are obsessed vit' findink Lockwood and the others, vit' killink them."

"I suppose I am." Calhoun felt no shame in it.

"Supposink somevon vas to come along and tell

you—vit' a convincink story—that Lockwood really vasn't the von responsible for killink the Fullers? Vhat vould you say to that?"

"I'd call the son of a bitch a liar, which is what he'd be, and then I'd put a bullet in . . ." He stopped and shook his head in annoyance. "I'm as bad as he is, ain't I."

Dutch Trude shrugged. "Men are like dot," she said simply, knowing from long experience.

"And women aren't?"

"Not about the same things."

"Are you obsessed with somethin'?" Calhoun asked, an odd feeling creeping over him. He suspected what she would answer, and he was not sure he wanted to hear it. On the other hand, he wasn't sure he didn't want to hear it either.

"Yah." Dutch Trude drew in a breath and eased it out. The time of reckoning seemed to be upon her. She figured that one way or the other, she would know in just a few moments exactly where she stood with Calhoun. "You," she finally admitted, body tense.

It was the answer Calhoun had both dreaded and wanted. Now that it was out in the open, he wasn't sure what to do with it. He worried about it, worried that someone would want him so deeply. It also pleased him, though, to know that he could still make a woman feel that way. "That's a mighty fool thing to be obsessed with, woman," he finally allowed, not committing himself to anything.

"I don't think so. Does that bother you?"

"Some," Calhoun admitted.

"I can go avay, not bother you anymore."

"I don't want that."

"You vant me?" Dutch Trude asked, still nervous.

"Yep," Calhoun said easily. "But I ain't so sure I want you as much as you want me."

"Dot could be a problem," Dutch Trude allowed. "But maybe not. Now kiss me and make me at least think you vant me a lot."

"My pleasure, ma'am," Calhoun said as he did what she had requested.

After breakfast the next morning, Calhoun tied Fuller to the tree again. Then he rode out a little way, trying to find the outlaws' trail. He had no luck, though, and he figured they had not come this way.

"Then vhich way do we go?" Dutch Trude asked after Calhoun had returned and explained.

"North," Calhoun said firmly. "They've had enough trouble back in east Texas, so I don't think they'd want to go there. Out west—and not far—is real Comanche country. They could've gone south, I suppose, but I don't think so."

"Vhy not?"

Calhoun shrugged. "Just a hunch."

"A hunch?" Fuller snorted.

"I've come to trust my hunches, Mister Fuller. It's what's kept me alive for so many years, when so many have tried to change that." He paused. "Anyway, I think they went north."

"Vhat about northeast? There're towns that vay."

"The posse's that way, too," Calhoun said flatly.

# CHAPTER

# * 17 *

They moved slowly northward for a couple of days, not sure where to go. Of the few farms they came by, two had been devastated. They stopped and Calhoun patiently buried eight more people.

Fuller sat, still tied, watching Calhoun while he dug graves as carefully as he'd watched him ride. Such watchfulness had gone a fair way toward changing his mind some about Wade Calhoun. He was now almost convinced of Calhoun's innocence in the slayings of his parents. There was no way Calhoun could have been responsible for all the carnage they were seeing now; the bodies were too freshly killed. Fuller began to think that perhaps this Royce Laird and his men really were the bloodthirsty band of outlaws that Calhoun had said they were.

Still, he could not be absolutely sure. Not yet anyway. Not when he had been so certain that Calhoun was the guilty party. He needed more proof than just realizing that there was more than one heartless outlaw in Texas, more than one man with the viciousness and lack of conscience required to so readily kill women and children.

There was more to Calhoun, though, than just the fact that he patiently and without complaint took the time to bury the unfortunate victims of whatever bloodthirsty band had been this way. Fuller had learned over the past few days that Calhoun was not the kind of man he associated with mindless violence. Yes, he could be as deadly as any man alive, Fuller figured. Any man who would walk into a crowded saloon ready to face down seven hardened gunmen all on his own had to be one tough *hombre.*

Yet the little violence that Fuller had seen Calhoun perpetrate always seemed to have a reason behind it. He was sure that any other outlaw would have killed him if he had insulted and challenged them the way he had Calhoun. Yet he had retained his coolness, even though Fuller knew the drifter was angry.

For his part, Calhoun was growing more frustrated. He knew the posse was still out after them, and that was annoying enough. But to keep getting close to Laird and Lockwood and the others and yet not be able to resolve this situation was even worse. Adding to it all was their discovery of more and more bodies, all killed by Laird's gang, Calhoun figured.

Then there was the omnipresent heat. Since the day Calhoun had left the Fullers' farm, there had been no rain, not even any clouds to break the sun's malignant presence and staggering heat. The sun's rays pelted down on them unmercifully, making them weary and lethargic. They moved as best they could from water hole to creek. Many of the water courses were dry or almost so, though the small group usually managed to find at least a little water wherever they went.

Calhoun also was troubled by his feelings for Dutch Trude, and even more so by her feelings for him. He generally was successful in keeping those thoughts out of his mind, since there was so much else to be concerned about. But the unwelcome thoughts intruded at times despite his efforts to keep them at bay. He wanted to forget about that until the matter of the Fullers' killers was resolved, but he was not as successful in forgetting as he would have liked to be.

Sometime during the afternoon, three days after leaving Luster, Calhoun and his two companions heard a gunshot, followed moments later by another. Calhoun galloped up to Dutch Trude, slid off his horse, and threw her the reins. Then he ran up a small incline and peered over. He watched for only a moment before sliding down the hill.

"Vhat is it?" Dutch Trude asked when Calhoun had reached the bottom.

"Comanches," Calhoun said flatly. "Looks like six of 'em. They just shot a couple buffalo about a quarter mile away."

"What're we gonna do?" Fuller asked. He was scared. Comanches were Indians he did not want to mess with. He had encountered them before, and had gotten away with his life. He had no desire to tempt fate again if he could help it.

"You two're gonna wait here. I'm goin' back up there and keep a watch on them boys."

"What'll happen if they head over this way?" Fuller asked nervously.

"We're gonna get in a fight," Calhoun said, sounding as if Fuller had lost his mind.

"I sure hope it don't come to that," Fuller said without embarrassment.

"Me, too," Calhoun agreed as he trotted back up the little hill to lay there. He watched for an hour as the Comanches leisurely butchered out some meat from the buffalo. They laughed and whooped, and from a distance appeared to eat some of the meat raw, carved right from the carcasses.

Calhoun wished he could go kill the Comanches. He hated all Indians—had since the Sioux had killed Lizbeth and Lottie—and as often as not he would try to kill them as soon as he saw them. But such a thing would be completely foolish right now, so he settled for watching.

Finally the Comanches loaded some meat on a few stolen—at least Calhoun figured they were stolen—horses and then mounted their ponies. They rode off, heading south-southeast.

Calhoun continued to watch until the Indians were out of sight, and even until the small amount of dust their ponies kicked up was gone. He stood and shaded his eyes with his hands and looked in a circle, taking his time. He saw no other signs that anyone else was around.

The saddle tramp trotted down the hill. "They're

gone," he said as he mounted his bay horse. He rode swiftly around the hillock toward the buffalo carcasses. Buzzards were already circling overhead, but Calhoun was glad to see that the wolves and coyotes had not shown up yet. He stopped and looked at Fuller. "You know how to butcher buffalo, Jethro?" he asked.

"Can't be much different from butcherin' cattle," Fuller said, shrugging.

Calhoun nodded. "You want some fresh meat for your supper tonight, go butcher us up some."

"Why don't you do it?" Fuller was still annoyed at being tied up all the time, and at having to take orders from Calhoun. He resisted as often as he could.

"Because I'm gonna be keepin' a watch out in case those goddamn Comanches come back," Calhoun said sourly.

Fuller looked at him in surprise. "You've had trouble with Comanches?" he asked.

"Not really," Calhoun said after considering for a few moments not answering. "In my case, it was Sioux who caused the most trouble." He spit into the dusty earth. "Killed my wife and our baby girl. I've hated Indians—all kinds—ever since."

Fuller nodded. He could understand that. It also gave him a little more respect for Calhoun. "You'll have to let me loose from these ropes," he said.

"I planned to," Calhoun said. "Do I need to warn you?" he asked as he rode up to Fuller.

"No, goddammit," Fuller said, trying to fight back the sudden surge of surliness.

Calhoun untied the ropes binding Fuller's hands and then handed him the big bowie knife.

Fuller took it and dismounted. He appreciated the freedom, although he knew he could go nowhere. He wouldn't even try, not with the deadly Calhoun mounted and watchful, and especially with those Comanches still out there somewhere.

While Fuller went about his work, Calhoun sat on his horse and watched carefully. He smoked a cigarette.

Fuller soon had some meat cut out and wrapped in a couple hunks of buffalo hide. As he tied them to the packhorse, he said, "Those redskins took the best cuts."

Calhoun nodded. "I expected. They leave anything edible?"

"Sure. There's some good hump meat and a bit of the ribs. Some others."

"It'll be nice for a change to haff some fresh meat," Dutch Trude said.

"Beggin' your pardon, ma'am," Fuller said. "I don't mean to say anything unkind, but with your poor cookin' skills, it don't matter much whether it's fresh buffalo or salted beef, I'd dare to say."

Dutch Trude's eyes danced heatedly. "I suppose your vife's a good cook," she offered.

"Yes, ma'am, she is."

"There's other things a woman can be good at, you know," Dutch Trude countered.

"My wife's pretty good at some of them things, too, ma'am," Fuller said, face reddening up in embarrassment.

"I'd argue that, Mister Fuller," she said stiffly. Then she shrugged. "But you're right, I am a poor cook. Alas, my talents lie elsevhere."

"And damn good talents they are, too, I'd say," Fuller said gallantly, though his face got even more red. He mounted his horse and turned to Calhoun. "Get your ropes, Mister Calhoun," he said quietly, glumly.

"You aimin' to give me any trouble if I leave you loose?" Calhoun asked.

"No," Fuller answered, surprised.

"Then let's move on."

"You believe me?" Fuller asked, surprised again.

"You give me your word?"

"I do."

"Then I believe you. A man who don't live up to his word ain't much of a man to my thinkin'," Calhoun said. "And I don't figure that Jess and Millie Fuller raised no children who'd not live up to their word. Now move on."

Fuller sat there a few seconds, staring at Calhoun in disbelief. He was half certain that Calhoun was going to shoot him in the back while they rode, but he could see no reason why Calhoun would do that. Not when he could've done the same thing anytime in the three days since they'd left Luster. He shrugged, accepting Calhoun at his word this time. He rode off, following Dutch Trude, as he always did.

Calhoun decided not to tie Fuller that night, either. "I'm still holdin' you to your word, Mister Fuller," he said as he and Dutch Trude turned in.

"You think that vas vise?" Dutch Trude asked as they lay down on their bedrolls.

Calhoun shrugged into the darkness. "I believe he'll live up to his word. If he don't, well . . ." He shrugged again. Calhoun was fairly certain that if Fuller tried anything, he would wake and be able to stop it. Fuller wasn't the most graceful of men, and Calhoun relied on an inner sense that seemed to wake him anytime trouble seemed about to happen.

Fuller lay on his own bedroll, wondering if he should try to escape. He thought he might be able to get to his horse. Even if he didn't take his saddle, he figured he could get to the horse and ride off into the night. He could be miles away before Calhoun awoke, he supposed. Trouble with such a plan was that Calhoun was right—Jess and Millie Fuller hadn't raised their children to give their word and then break it for their own convenience.

Plus, Fuller was almost certain now that Calhoun was innocent of killing his parents. He still had a little bit of a hard time accepting that thought, but it seemed to be the correct one. Mainly he figured that if Calhoun was as bloodthirsty as he had thought, the saddle tramp would have killed him a long time ago. Fuller could see no reason for Calhoun to keep him alive, especially for three full days. He sighed, deciding that he would worry about escaping some other time. Then he let himself drift off to sleep.

Early the next afternoon, Calhoun began to feel the itch between his shoulders again. "Shit," he whispered. He didn't know which would be worse, to find that the posse was back on his trail, or to learn that the small Comanche war party was following him and his two companions.

There was no place he could see to really hide, so

he rode on, not alerting his companions yet. An hour later, he saw dust to the east. It looked to be coming from a sizable group, which he figured would let the Comanches out, unless they had met some others of their tribe.

Calhoun finally called a halt near another of the interminable hills in the region. This one ran for a couple of miles, it seemed, in a roughly northeast-southwest fashion, a long, skinny, not very high, wadded-up blanket of short, dry grass that ran off toward the horizon in two directions.

He climbed up the wavering hill and took a look around. He could see a group of horsemen coming hard from the southeast. He assumed it was Packard's posse. In a way, he admired the marshal's tenacity.

The hill he was on was not very good defensively, but he spotted one behind him, roughly to the west. He estimated it was two miles away. There was nothing between this hill and that one, except flat, scrubby prairie. There were also no real hills or hiding places for a mile or more north and south. It would have to do.

Calhoun went down the hill, mounted, and pointed toward the other hill. "Ride!" he said.

When they got to the hill, they rode straight up one side and down the other. At the bottom, they dismounted. Since this was to be a veritable duplicate of the last stand they had made against the posse, Calhoun said, "You ready, Trude?"

Dutch Trude nodded, smiling at him. For some reason, she was fairly sure they were going to die today. She didn't care, though. She was with the man she loved. Yes, loved. She was finally able to admit that to herself. She was sure Calhoun didn't feel the same, but she knew he liked her more than a little. The other might come with time—if they got any more time. If they didn't, she could die happy alongside her man.

"What about me?" Fuller asked quietly.

That posed a problem for Calhoun. He figured that maybe he should tie Fuller up good and tight and leave him here down at the bottom of the hill. Fuller had not tried anything, though, and so Calhoun was loath to do that. Now he wondered just what he *should* do about Jethro Fuller.

Sensing Calhoun's uncertainty, Fuller asked, "Can I make a suggestion, Mister Calhoun?"

Calhoun looked at him for some moments, then nodded slowly.

# CHAPTER 18

"You can let me go," Fuller said solemnly. "I can ride out there and meet the posse—if that's what it is." The last was something of a question.

Calhoun nodded. "Seems to be."

"I can talk to them, tell 'em to go back to Pecan Grove or wherever they're from."

"And just why would you go and do that?" Calhoun asked suspiciously.

Fuller looked humbled. "I don't really think you killed Ma and Pa," he said, bringing his eyes up to meet Calhoun's. "I can't be a hundred percent sure, you understand, but I'm pretty well convinced you didn't do it."

"That's what I've been tellin' you all along," Calhoun said flatly. "When did you have this great revelation?"

Fuller shrugged. "It didn't come to me all at once.

And I still ain't fully sure, but it was a matter of watchin' you. How you act, what kind of man you are close up. It's one thing to hear that someone killed your folks—you know, I couldn't help but believe it, especially after seein' you." He shrugged again. "It's another thing travelin' with a feller and learnin' things about him."

It all sounded plausible to Calhoun. Besides, he couldn't see keeping Fuller around much longer anyway, no matter what Fuller planned to do. He could kill Fuller, but that went against the grain. Fuller had really done nothing to him, and Calhoun could not hate Fuller for having wanted to kill him. It had made sense for Fuller to think that Calhoun had killed his parents.

Calhoun jerked his head. "Go on."

Fuller was surprised, and asked, "You sure?"

"Yep."

"You ain't gonna shoot me in the back, are you?" Fuller asked, suddenly worried.

"Nope. My word." If Calhoun was capable of smiling, he might have done so then at the look on Fuller's face.

Fuller nodded. "Can I take my horse?" he asked.

"Sure. But I'll keep your revolver. A man like you is likely to get in trouble if he's packin' a pistol." He paused. "You mind a word of advice?"

"I don't mind you givin' it," Fuller said evenly. "Don't mean I'm gonna take it."

Calhoun nodded and rolled a cigarette. Once he had it fired up, he said, "I'd avoid the posse if I was you. I'd wager hard cash that those boys ain't gonna be all that friendly to you, especially if you really tell 'em that you don't think I'm the guilty party anymore."

"They'll be all right."

Calhoun shrugged. He thought Fuller was a damn fool if he still planned to do what he had said he would, but that was no longer his problem. "And another thing. A Mister Bockmeister, who owns the general store in Pecan Grove, is holdin' some money due your folks. Money for produce I brought in for 'em. I reckon it's yours now. Make sure you collect it."

"I will," Fuller said with a nod. He turned to leave.

"I'd be obliged if you didn't tell 'em exactly where we are," Calhoun said.

"I won't."

"And, Mister Fuller," Calhoun said, as Fuller mounted his horse, "if I see you ridin' with them posse men, I'm gonna shoot you first."

Fuller nodded. "I won't ride with 'em. My word." He smiled wearily. "Well, Mister Calhoun, Miss Trude, I can't say as it's been a pleasure travelin' with you."

Calhoun turned and began walking up the hill as Fuller rode off. Dutch Trude followed her man, the reloading supplies in hand.

Calhoun and Dutch Trude sat on top of the hill, which spread out to their left and right. They watched out across the little valley, waiting. Far off to their right—roughly south—they could see Fuller riding at a good clip toward the lower part of the opposite hill. Then he disappeared over the crest, and the two were alone. Heat poured down from the sun, and the wind shoved at their backs.

"Vhy don't ve take off, Vade?" Dutch Trude asked.

Calhoun shrugged. "Where could we go?" he countered.

"Ve could outrun them, just the two of us."

"Scared?"

"Yah. But not for vhy you might think. I'm afraid to die when I've just discovered how deeply I care for you. I vant to see that through to the end."

"You will," Calhoun responded, lips twitching a little. "It just won't be as long as you might've thought."

"That is the problem. I vant to be vit' you for a good long time."

"That might be a problem," Calhoun conceded. "Besides, you could be wrong about your feelin's for me." He wasn't sure how he felt about that.

"Vhy do you say that?" Dutch Trude asked, alarmed.

"You felt the same way about Laird at one time," Calhoun said quietly. He realized that the thought of such a thing pained him more than he wanted to admit.

"Yah. I thought so, too," Dutch Trude said, voice heavy with shame. "But I didn't." She sighed and wiped away a tear. "I can understand it if you don't vant me, after the sinful life I've lived. Once ve get all this bad business taken care of—if ve live through it all—I'll leave you be."

Calhoun looked over at Dutch Trude. Her face was stricken, and tears rolled down her plump, pretty cheeks. Calhoun cared for Dutch Trude more in that moment than he had about any woman since Lizbeth had died. He was not sure the feeling would last—wasn't even sure if he *wanted* it to last—but he did know there would be more to their relationship. If they lived.

"I never said I wanted that," he pointed out. "All I was doin' was pointin' out a fact from your past. I don't want you gettin' mixed up with the wrong man again. You've been hurt enough."

"You think you're the wrong man for me?" she asked.

"Might be. I ain't ever been good for any folks. The Fullers learned that the hard way."

"Vell," Dutch Trude said with conviction, "I think you're the right man for me." She rested a damp cheek on Calhoun's shirt. "Do you vant me around?" she asked hopefully.

"For a while at least," he said honestly.

"Dot's all a girl can ask."

They sat that way for a while before Dutch Trude finally dried her face and blew her nose on the hem of her dress. It was the best she could do under the circumstances, and though the dress was little more than a week or so old, it was already showing heavy signs of wear. A little snot on the hem wouldn't hurt it any.

It was almost two hours before the posse rode swiftly over the hill across the little valley and headed toward them. When the posse was half a mile away, Calhoun swore.

"Vhat's wrong?" Dutch Trude asked.

"That son of a bitch marshal from Luster is with Packard. Looks like he brought some of his boys with him, too."

"Shit," Calhoun repeated when the posse men were less than a quarter mile away. "Fuller's ridin' with 'em, too." He sighed. "Probably never should've trusted that son of a bitch."

"Vait," Dutch Trude suddenly said. "I don't think he's really ridink *vit'* them."

Calhoun stared across the distance, then caught a glance of sunlight off something. "I'll be damned," he muttered, "they did arrest the poor bastard."

A few moments later, Calhoun said, "Best get below the ridge top here." He lay prone, extending out both arms—each holding a fully loaded Dragoon—to use the ground as a brace. Since this situation was almost an exact duplicate of the one he faced in his previous gun battle with the posse, Calhoun did not want to give the men much of a chance, especially since the posse had been reinforced by men from Luster. When the first of the posse men were about seventy-five yards off, Calhoun began firing.

Through the cloud of bluish white powder smoke, he could see horses and men falling. A few got up, a few others did not. One that he had aimed for right from the start was Marshal Johnny Buford. He was rather satisfied when he saw Buford go sailing off his horse and bounce along the ground.

Calhoun tossed his Dragoons to Dutch Trude and snatched up Goodrich's revolver, which he had taken back from Dutch Trude earlier, and Fuller's pistol. He fired again, smoothly and steadily, using a pistol in each hand.

More men and horses went down, but the posse men were fleeing, racing to get out of range, leaving their dead and dying behind. They finally stopped and dismounted. One man watched over the horses.

The others quickly flung themselves down on the ground.

Up on the hill, Calhoun squiggled backward a little, until he reached Dutch Trude. She had finished reloading the Dragoons, and swiftly did the same to the two other pistols. When she was done, Calhoun said, "Let's get out of here."

"Vhere're ve goink?" Dutch Trude asked, unconcerned by the prospect of being on the move again.

Calhoun shrugged. "I want to try to find a better place to hole up. Fightin' out here in the open like this ain't to my likin'."

"You think they'll be after us soon?"

Calhoun shrugged again. "Can't tell. I know I killed at least a few of 'em. That'll slow 'em down. Because there's no cover between where they are and this hill, they'll stay put a while. They know what I can do. They might work up enough nerve to charge on horseback, but I figure they'll wait till dark for that. We can be miles from here by then."

"So, let's go."

They rode off slowly, not wanting to kick up any dust, and headed almost due west. Two miles or so away, Calhoun swung them northward, and they picked up speed. They avoided a ranch they spotted in the distance late in the afternoon and pressed on.

They continued to ride until past dark, since they had found no place with any cover to stop. With the light of the moon and the many stars, they could see pretty well, and so they continued.

Calhoun estimated it was about midnight when he heard the slight rippling of a creek and foliage ruffling in the wind. "Wait here," he whispered. "I want to make sure there're no surprises by the creek."

Dutch Trude nodded. She was a little worried. Thoughts of Comanches lying in wait in the brush filled her mind.

Calhoun was gone only a few minutes. "Everything's clear," he said.

"Is a fire all right?" Dutch Trude asked as they moved into the thickets along the creek.

"I expect," Calhoun said. "You that hungry?"

"Yah. And I think you are, too. You need food to keep up your strength."

"Just keep it small," Calhoun said. "Maybe dig a pit for it, too. That way it won't be seen too far."

Before long, they had their small camp set up and their chores done. They sat together, trying to relax while slapping away gnats and mosquitoes, waiting for their supper.

They ate quietly and with little enthusiasm. The many days on the trail, the constant movement, the frequent harassment, the frustration of not being able to complete the mission that they had set for themselves all combined to wear on them. They fell asleep soon afterward, lulled by the wind in the brush.

Another sound in the brush woke Calhoun, who figured it was just before dawn as he rolled out of his bedroll, a Dragoon in his hand. He crouched in the darkness, waiting. Then he saw a shadow moving, a shadow not caused by foliage. He rose and moved swiftly, around some brush and a tree, when he suddenly became aware that he was right behind a man. Another step and he would've walked right into him, though the newcomer seemed not to know he was there.

Calhoun thumbed back the hammer of the Dragoon, and the shadowy man froze. "Lookin' for somethin'?" Calhoun asked quietly.

"That you, Calhoun?" the man countered.

"Jethro?" Calhoun responded, confused.

"Yep."

"What the hell're you doin' here, boy?" Calhoun was rather taken aback by this development. He also was suddenly worried. While Fuller seemed to have been handcuffed with the posse, that might have been strictly a ruse. The whole posse—or what was left of it—might be just outside the brush, waiting to kill him and Dutch Trude.

"Lookin' for you."

Calhoun's concern deepened. "You alone?"

"Hell, yes. Who'd I be with out here . . ." Fuller stopped, then nodded. "Ah, yes, I see. The last you saw me, I was ridin' off to meet the posse."

"Actually," Calhoun said flatly, "the last time I saw you, you were ridin' with the posse, chargin' toward the hill where I was." He paused, letting that sink in. "Now, can you give me one reason why I shouldn't just blow your head off here and now?"

"I'm here to help you," Fuller said. "I swear." He sighed, deciding to take the risk. He turned. "I give you my word, Mister Calhoun, that I'm here alone and that I want to help you. I have some information you might be able to use." He sighed again. He was not used to all this violence and death. "If you don't believe me, or if you don't think my word is good, then go ahead and kill me." He was ready to wet his pants at the very thought.

# CHAPTER

# * 19 *

Calhoun brought Fuller back to the camp and tied him up. Waking Dutch Trude, he left her to watch over Fuller, then went on a scout. He found no one else, and so he returned to the camp and untied Fuller. By then, dawn had risen, and the light fog from the creek was already burning off.

"So?" Calhoun questioned.

"You were right about the posse, Wade," Fuller said over coffee, bacon, and biscuits that Dutch Trude had made while Calhoun was gone. Fuller didn't seem to mind the taste this time. He figured it was probably because he had come so close to really dying this time. "I was arrested by Marshal Buford. That's why you saw me ridin' with the posse."

"You vere handcuffed, yah?" Dutch Trude asked.

"Yep. How'd you know?" Fuller was only a little surprised. He was getting used to the surprises Calhoun and Dutch Trude sprang on people.

"Thought we saw 'em," Calhoun answered.

"You did."

"Why'd that asshole arrest you?"

"Claimed I was aidin' and abettin' you two in your criminal enterprises," Fuller said flatly. "Was he to arrest me again now, he'd be right."

"Tell it all," Calhoun ordered quietly.

"I found them fairly quickly. They saw me comin' and stopped to wait. Soon's I got there, I told Marshal Buford and Marshal Packard that they were after the wrong man for killin' my folks."

Neither was inclined to believe Fuller. "You're a lyin' son of a bitch," Buford said flatly.

"I am not," Fuller responded defensively.

"Then how the hell did you come to the conclusion that the murderous son of a bitch Wade Calhoun isn't the one who killed your folks?" Buford demanded.

"Because I've been ridin' with him since he left Luster. He told me it was men from Royce Laird's gang, whoever they are, who killed my folks. I didn't believe him at first, but as we rode, we saw the handiwork of Laird's men—or some others. At least two farms we saw had dead folks left by someone, and it couldn't have been Calhoun."

"Boy, you are one dumb bastard to be took in by the lies of a man like this Calhoun feller. You saw what he did in Luster."

"The only one I was took in by was him," Fuller said, pointing to Packard, "when he filled my head full of tales of all the wrongdoin' that Calhoun supposedly did."

"I don't take bein' called a liar lightly, son," Packard growled.

"Then you shouldn't lie, Marshal. You . . ."

"How'd you end up ridin' with him?" Buford interjected.

"I was fixin' to kill him, since I believed Marshal Packard and thought he'd killed Ma and Pa. But he got the drop on me, and took me his prisoner."

"Hell, I had the drop on him, boy. I was all ready . . . goddamn and saints preserve me," Buford snapped. "It was you who near split my melon open when I had Calhoun caught dead to rights, wasn't it?"

"Yessir. You see, I wanted to be the one who killed him. . . ."

"Like a donkey's ass, you wanted to kill him," Buford snarled. "You either was in cahoots with him, or you wanted the reward all to yourself. Seein' as what happened after, includin' him sendin' you here to plead for his freedom, I'd wager it was the first all along."

"That's a goddamn, bald-faced lie, Marshal," Fuller sputtered, realizing he had made a mistake approaching the posse, that he should have stayed with Calhoun and Dutch Trude.

"You're under arrest, boy," Buford said nastily. "For aidin' an outlaw in his criminal pursuits, and for knockin' the duly sworn marshal of Luster, Texas, on the head and leavin' me to die on a saloon floor. I ain't a forgivin' man when such things happen."

"But . . ."

"Shut the hell up," Buford snapped. After one of the other men clapped handcuffs on Fuller's wrists, Buford asked, "Now, where's that murderin' son of a bitch holed up?"

"I ain't sure," Fuller said sullenly. "Last I saw him, Calhoun was ridin' near due west from a point a little southwest of here."

"You know, boy," Buford said, "if you'd cooperate with us, the judge might see fit to go easy on you once your time for sentencin' comes up. Now, where is Calhoun?"

"That whore still ridin' with him?" Packard interjected.

"I didn't see no whore," Fuller said evenly.

"Lyin' bastard," Packard muttered as he walked away.

"And I told you where the last place I saw Calhoun was, Marshal," Fuller added, looking at Buford. He could not believe that he had allowed himself to think that this pitiful excuse for a lawman would help him.

Buford rose. "We'll ride northwest," he announced.

"Now, wait a goddamn minute, Johnny," Packard said tensely. "This here's my posse. I give the orders."

"Some posse," Buford sneered. "You been chasin' that asshole for what, two weeks? More? You caught up to him once and he shot the shit out of your men. I'm a former Texas Ranger, goddammit," he added with undisguised pride. "I'm takin' over, so's I can make sure things turn out right this time. We're closer to my jurisdiction anyway."

Packard thought to argue, but then realized it would be futile. The important thing was catching Calhoun. And Dutch Trude. He wanted to get his hands on the prostitute after what she had done to him back in Pecan Grove. Not only the knock on the head, but the deception. He was still infuriated by that. "All right, Marshal," he said in conciliatory tones. "As long as I get to take him back to Pecan Grove for the hangin'."

"You can have him," Buford said. "I just want to make sure he gets caught."

"A question, though?" Packard added. When Buford nodded, Packard asked, "Why northwest?"

"That's the way that bastard was headin' before. I can't see no reason why he'd change directions now. Especially since we're gettin' mighty close to Comanche country. Besides, I don't believe a goddamn word this peckerwood tells me." He jerked a thumb in Fuller's direction. "Let's ride."

A few hours later, they rode into a fusillade of bullets that left a number of them out in the open. The others raced far enough back to be well out of range of even a rifle, and took stock. Buford was down, as were four other men. One of those was painfully making his way toward those who were left. Six horses had gone down, but two had made it back up and were also wandering back. The other four whinnied in pain and fright.

"What do we do now, Marshal?" Frankie Kitchell asked. He had been with the posse right from the beginning, and was among the most eager to catch Calhoun. He still hated Calhoun for having beaten him up in front of everyone in Hanney's saloon.

"We sit and wait," Packard said. His stomach was a mess, churning with acid brought on by worry. He had lost nearly half a dozen of his own men on this mission, and that was not going to be an easy thing to explain to the good people of Pecan Grove. Especially if he came back without Calhoun—or at least Calhoun's corpse.

Fuller got edgy after an hour, but he stuck it out another twenty minutes. Then he stood and went to his horse. He mounted up and started riding back toward the battlefield.

"Hey, where the hell're you goin'?" Packard demanded.

"Out there," Fuller said.

"You're a prisoner."

"I'm Buford's prisoner, not yours."

"It ain't safe out there."

"Maybe not. But I figure Calhoun won't shoot me. If he does, then you don't have to worry about me anymore."

"And if he doesn't shoot you?"

"Then I'm goin' home to my family, Marshal. You want to stop me, you're welcome to try to do so." He turned his horse and trotted out toward Buford's body. There, he dismounted and found that Buford was still alive, though he didn't look very good. "Where's the key to the handcuffs, Marshal?" he asked.

Buford gasped, but no words came out.

Fuller searched for the key. In doing so, he encountered a small ornament of carved buffalo horn hanging around Buford's neck. He tensed as his fingers touched it. "Where'd you get this necklace?" he asked tightly.

"My wife's cousin Royce give it to me," Buford wheezed. "Why?" He figured Fuller just wanted to steal it.

"It was my mother's, you son of a bitch," Fuller snarled. He jerked it free and shoved it in his shirt pocket. "That means your goddamn kin killed my folks, and you tried to protect 'em, you bastard." He paused, trying to think. This was of great importance, that much he knew, but he figured there was more information he could get. He simply didn't know what to ask. Then it dawned on him. "Where're Laird and the others headin'?"

"North-northwest," Buford gasped. He said nothing more for some moments, struggling to catch his breath. Then he said, "Town called Branchwater." He fell silent again, his chest heaving spastically.

Fuller continued his search, moving with urgency now. He finally found the key, then undid the handcuffs and tossed them aside. Fuller stood, aching to kill Buford, but knowing his conscience wouldn't let him. He looked around and spotted the lawman's pistol. He retrieved it and checked it. Seeing that it was loaded and ready to go, he shoved it into the waistband of his trousers. He went back and pulled off Buford's belt, with the pouch of paper cartridges and such. Then he mounted his horse and rode off.

To throw off suspicion, he headed south between the two hills. But three miles or so away, he crossed over the hill to the west, in almost the same spot as he had crossed the other way not so long ago. Then he galloped to the place where he had left Calhoun and Dutch Trude. He did not see their horses, and figured they had taken off. To be sure, though, he climbed to the top of the hill. He lay down and looked around, but did not see them.

Not knowing which way they had gone—and

being completely unable to read trail signs of any kind—Fuller mounted up again and rode northwest. He had tried to throw the posse off when he had told Buford that Calhoun had been heading west. He had been horrified to hear Buford decide against that direction. Now he figured Buford was probably right: Calhoun most likely had kept heading northwest. Fuller decided he would do the same.

He rode on, not moving too fast, since he was not sure where he was going and he didn't want to attract attention. Still, he didn't go too slowly either; he didn't want the posse catching up to him. He had no food or anything, so he couldn't see stopping for the night. Not when there was so much starlight and moonlight to travel by.

Hours and hours later, he spotted a low glimmer of light. He took it to be the embers of a fire, and he froze, frightened. The encounter with the Comanches the other day had kept those Indians in the forefront of his mind, and he was certain now that he had found a camp of them here. Of course, he reassured himself, it could just as easily be Calhoun and Dutch Trude out there along the creek he heard bubbling.

With a sigh, he dismounted and loosened his saddle to let the horse breathe. Then he stood there wondering what he should do next. He knew it would make the most sense to just ride for his home, back to his family, and forget all about this business. He found, though, that he could not do that. He simply had to make amends with Calhoun. It was an awful thing, he thought, to be absolutely certain that an innocent man was responsible for killing one's loved ones. He just had to find Calhoun and make things right, plus impart to him the kernel of information he had gotten from Buford about Laird and his men.

Then he decided: There was nothing else he could do but go out there and see if the camp was Calhoun's or the Comanches', or someone else's. Hell, for all he knew, it might not even be a campfire he had seen; it might've just been his tired vision playing tricks on him in the darkness. After all, he had seen the dull glow only intermittently.

He steeled himself, tightened the saddle just in case, and then walked on toward the unknown, holding the reins to the horse. When he reached some brush, he tied the horse. Taking a moment to make sure he had gathered all the courage he could muster, he pushed on through the brush toward the creek.

Some tense minutes later, he was about convinced that there were no Comanches about; indeed, he had about convinced himself that he had seen no campfire at all. He felt a great sense of relief. Then he heard a pistol cocking, and a cold, familiar voice asking, "Lookin' for somethin'?"

"So old Buford was wearin' your ma's necklace?" Calhoun said with a shake of his head. "Son of a bitch."

"That's right," Fuller said firmly. "When I saw it—and especially after he told me where he had gotten it—I knew for absolute certain that you hadn't killed my folks. I . . . I'd like to apologize for that. How could I ever think . . ."

"Forget it," Calhoun said uncomfortably.

"But I . . ."

Calhoun stood and walked off.

"Better to let it go, Mister Fuller," Dutch Trude said. "He has accepted your apology."

Fuller nodded.

# CHAPTER

# ★ 20 ★

"So when do we leave for Branchwater?" Fuller asked almost jauntily after he had filled himself with food and coffee and had finished telling his tale.

"Trude and me'll leave soon's we can get ready."

"What about me?" Fuller asked, surprised and even a little hurt. He had gone through a lot to help Calhoun—rightfully so, considering the way he had treated Calhoun at first. Still, he thought he would get to go along. He figured that since he had come this far, he might as well see the business through to the end.

"Best thing you can do, Jethro," Calhoun said evenly, "is go home. I've told you that before."

"But I want to go to Branchwater with you."

"You ain't no gunman," Calhoun said flatly. "You got grit, I'll say that much, but you're not used to dealing in the business that's ahead of me. I'm obliged for the help you've given, and for your offer of more. But your family needs you a lot more than Trude and I do."

"But . . ."

"Go home," Calhoun snapped. He was tired of the arguing and all the troubles he had faced in the past few weeks. It was well past due for getting this business finished. "Make sure your wife and kids are all right. Then go on to your folks' place and see what you want to do with it. You might even want to pay your respects to 'em."

Fuller realized with horror that he had not done so. He had planned to go to Pecan Grove and do that before chasing after Calhoun, whom he thought at the time was the killer. Then he had found Calhoun in Luster and this whole business had begun, with all its crazy turns. "Where are they?" he asked, voice low and pained.

"Under the big tree. Somebody from Pecan Grove made sure they were buried right. Preacher Maughm—at least that's what I think your ma called him—said words over 'em and all, from what I was told. All right and proper."

Fuller nodded. "You sure you don't need my help?" he asked, still torn between wanting to do what was right by his slain parents and going with Calhoun.

"I'm sure."

Dutch Trude suddenly leaned over and whispered urgently in Calhoun's ear. Then Calhoun shook his head. Dutch Trude argued some more, and Calhoun finally nodded, though he did not seem happy about it. "You can come with us, if you'd rather," Calhoun said almost evenly. He was annoyed that Dutch Trude had convinced him he was wrong.

Fuller was surprised again. "What changed your mind?"

"Trude's worried about you gettin' caught by the posse again. Or worse, the Comanches."

Fuller almost shuddered. "I'd rather not meet either of those if I'm by myself," he allowed.

Calhoun nodded. "Just make sure you keep out of the way when we get to Branchwater."

"I will," Fuller vowed. "My word on it."

They hurriedly cleaned up their little camp and saddled their horses. Just before leaving, Calhoun looked squarely at Fuller. "I'm puttin' my faith in your word, boy," he said, pointing to the pistol in Fuller's belt. It was the one Fuller had taken from Marshal Buford.

Fuller glanced down and nodded. "Have no fear from me on that account, Mister Calhoun," he said solemnly.

Calhoun nodded. "You won't mind, though, if I was to keep the gun I took from you a long time ago, would you?"

"Nope," Fuller said. "I figure you'll need it a lot more than I will if we—uh, I mean *you*—get into the fracas we expect to."

Calhoun nodded again.

Not long after the three had gotten back on the move, Calhoun picked up what he believed were signs of the outlaws, and they began following the trail. It was not hard to follow, and Calhoun figured the outlaws were not very concerned that someone might be following them. He thought it likely that Laird had either gotten word from Buford somehow that he didn't have to worry or was assuming that Buford would find Calhoun and the others and eliminate the problem of pursuit. Whichever, Calhoun figured it presumptuous on Laird's part, even arrogant. He hoped to use that to his advantage.

The land was generally more flat out here, though it still rolled some all the way to the horizon. It was drier, too, with short grass that was crisp from being without water for a while. Dust rose in little puffs each time one of the animals put a hoof down. The air was almost brittle, and the sun merciless. The heat threatened to smash them into little puddles; the dust caught in their throats, gagging them.

The three plodded stoically along, with Dutch Trude trailing the packhorse behind. In the late afternoon, less than an hour before dusk, they topped a barren ridge and saw a small, ramshackle ranch house down below. They stopped.

"Why'n hell would anyone come out here?" Fuller wondered.

"Because they're damn fools is why," Calhoun said roughly. "But if folks didn't do that, your ma and pa would've never had that nice place back by Pecan Grove."

"Reckon it *was* kind of empty back when they set down roots there," Fuller said. Despite his sadness, he was suddenly proud of his leather-tough, hardworking parents. He paused, as a sudden, horrible thought swept over him. "Laird's tracks lead right down there, don't they?" he asked.

"Yep," Calhoun said, spitting. It didn't work too well, since his mouth was so dry. "Shit," he muttered at the failed attempt.

"They're still down there, too, yah?" Dutch Trude interjected.

"Yep," Calhoun said again.

"Let's go get 'em, then," Fuller said. He was scared but determined to uphold his end of the work ahead.

"No," Calhoun said, surprising both Fuller and Dutch Trude. "It's too near dark."

"But that's good," Fuller said. "They won't be able to see us comin'."

Calhoun nodded. "That's true. But we wouldn't be able to see each other well either."

"Vhat's your plan, then?" Dutch Trude asked.

"We stay right where we're at for the night. Just before dawn, I'll head down to the house."

Fuller nodded, though he was a little skeptical. He said nothing about his doubts.

Dutch Trude also nodded. She preferred leaving such planning to Calhoun, since she trusted in him completely.

"It'll be a cold camp, and we probably won't get much sleep," Calhoun said. "But I suppose that's a hell of a lot better than ridin' down there now and gettin' blasted."

"Vhat if they leave during the night?" Dutch Trude asked.

"Then we'll have to go chasin' 'em again. I figure they're here at least for the night, though. If they were gonna move on, they likely would've done so already. They're probably glad to have a roof over their heads, and maybe some beds for sleeping."

They hobbled the horses on the side of the ridge away from the house. Calhoun and Fuller groomed the animals, then resaddled them; they might need the horses in a hurry, so Calhoun figured they had better be prepared. Then the three sat up on the ridge in the swiftly gathering darkness, gnawing at beef jerky and sipping stagnant water from their canteens.

When darkness was full on them, and before the moon and stars had really spread any light, Calhoun said, "You might as well get some sleep, Jethro."

Fuller nodded and stretched out where he was. Though he was scared, he managed to fall asleep quickly.

When Calhoun heard Fuller begin to snore, he said, "You can get some sleep, too, Trude."

"Yah, that would be goot." She kissed Calhoun, then lay down at a right angle to him, with her head in his lap. Calhoun stroked her hair until she, too, fell asleep.

With the growing moonlight and starlight, Calhoun could keep an eye on the house. After a while there was little activity. Twice he heard a woman scream down in the house, and he figured the outlaws were sporting with one of the women who lived there. It would not be pleasant for the woman—or women. Each time the scream was heard, Dutch Trude rustled and came partially awake. He calmed her with soothing words and a soft touch on her face or hair, and she settled back into sleep.

Occasionally Calhoun rolled a cigarette and lit it, not caring if anyone in the house looked up the hill and saw it. He figured they would not believe their eyes anyway, and that if they did, it would make them wonder. Having them spooked might work to his advantage.

When he judged it was less than an hour before dawn, he roused Dutch Trude, and then Fuller.

After taking a minute to rub the tiredness from his eyes, Fuller went down the hill, got the horses, and brought them back. They all mounted up.

"I'm ready," Fuller said firmly.

"Yah, me too."

"You're stayin' here," Calhoun said. "Both of you."

"Like hell I am," Fuller snapped. Now that he had set this task before himself, he was not about to be denied. "I come with you to help, and, by God, that's what I'm going to do."

"You can be the biggest help by stayin' out of my way. Like you promised to do."

"I promised to stay out of your way in Branchwater," Fuller reminded him.

"Maybe this ain't Branchwater," Calhoun responded, "but the idea's the same. Besides, I need you to watch over Trude so's she don't get hurt. That's important to me."

"I don't need . . ." Dutch Trude started. She clapped her mouth shut when Calhoun turned a forbidding look her way.

"She don't think she needs anyone," Calhoun went on evenly. "But she does. And I'll be obliged if you watched over her. I'd be mighty put out was somethin' to happen to her."

"I'll watch over her good," Fuller said. He was relieved that he wouldn't have to go down there and face six or seven outlaws. On the other hand, he was not happy about being left alone with Dutch Trude. If something happened to Calhoun, which seemed likely considering the odds, he would have to try to get the woman across half of central Texas to safety. That was bad enough, but he would have a posse, some Comanches, and maybe even the outlaws as a barrier to the completion of that mission.

"You remember that fold of land over there?" Calhoun asked, pointing. When Fuller nodded, Calhoun said, "You and Trude go there and wait. It looks to be about the safest place around, and you'll be able to keep a watch on that ranch from over there. You see somethin' happen to me, you two ride like hell."

"I vill not," Dutch Trude said firmly. "I vill come to you."

"You'll ride like hell," Calhoun snapped. "There ain't no use in you gettin' yourself killed just so's you can come weep over my swellin' carcass."

"But . . ."

"You just do what I said," Calhoun snarled. "Of course, I don't mind none if you was to wish that doesn't become necessary."

"I'd even pray for it," Dutch Trude said with a sad smile, "if I knew any prayers."

"I know a couple," Fuller said. "Come, Miss Trude, let's go and leave Wade to his work."

Dutch Trude moved closer to Calhoun, then leaned over and unabashedly kissed him hard on the mouth. "You vatch yourself, mine man," she said after she pulled her lips away.

Calhoun nodded. "Go." He was a little irritated at

the kiss. Not that he hadn't enjoyed it, but it had taken his mind off the work at hand, even if just a little. As the other two rode off, he took a few moments to compose himself again, to prepare the anger inside him so that his fighting edge would be finely honed.

Finally he began riding down the hill, moving slowly, trying to lessen the jolts to his buttocks a little. Then he was on the flats. He had fixed the scene in his mind yesterday afternoon, before darkness had covered the land. The house was almost dead ahead. It was a small, almost pitiful looking building. To his left, separated from the house by several yards, was a good-sized barn and a corral. There were a number of horses and cattle in the barn. Calhoun had also seen cattle grazing over a large area. A small creek ran on the right, close to the house and right through the center of a garden patch. Calhoun had been a little surprised to not hear a dog barking, and to hear only a few chickens raising a ruckus, until he realized that the outlaws probably had killed those animals.

He reached the corral and dismounted, then tied the reins to the top rail of the corral fence—a weak-seeming enclosure made of thin rails. He walked to the barn—a solid structure made mostly of sod—and went inside. He stopped and waited a few moments for his eyes to adjust to the blackness. Then he began looking around. He nodded in satisfaction when he saw his saddle.

Calhoun carried the saddle outside where he could see and carefully check it, making sure it was in good shape. Then he took out the two big Colt

Walkers from the saddle holsters and looked them over. They had been used, but had been relatively well taken care of, and they were loaded. He slipped them back into the saddle holsters.

Unhurried, he also checked his rifle and shotgun. He considered bringing the latter with him, but he decided it would get in his way inside the house. He returned it to the scabbard.

He pulled the stolen saddle off his bay horse and then put on the fancy saddle he had had for years. That done, he walked to the house. There was a small porch of sorts, and he stepped up onto it and rolled a cigarette. He lit it and then waited for the day to break.

# CHAPTER

# * 21 *

The house looked a lot more shoddy up close than it had from a distance. The rickety two-story structure was made mostly of small, twisted logs, and Calhoun figured there must have been a grove of scrub oak or live oak around somewhere. The spacious cracks between the thin logs had been chinked with sod and mud, much of which had dried and fallen out. The small porch on which Calhoun stood sagged, and Calhoun was not sure it would hold his weight. He also wondered if the porch roof would fall on his head at any moment.

The area reeked of cattle and chicken dung, stagnant creek water, old mud, dust, and the flat, acrid odor blown toward him from the outhouse.

A cock crowed, and Calhoun flipped his cigarette butt away into the dust. He drew his two Dragoons and was about ready to kick in the door when he heard horses galloping. He glanced around and swore when he saw Packard and his posse riding hell-bent down the small hill toward the house. There looked to be only a half-dozen of the men left.

"Shit," Calhoun muttered again. He figured he had better get the first job over with—taking care of Laird and his men—before turning his attention to the posse.

He kicked the door off the hinges and stepped inside, finding himself in the kitchen. It was dark, but the open doorway and a low-burning lantern provided a little light—just not enough to let him see the body just inside the doorway. He stumbled over it as he moved inside, and he cursed silently.

The posse's rush woke the house, though, and fire suddenly spit out of the darkness from a back corner of the room, between the stove and a battered old cabinet.

Calhoun hissed as a bullet slapped off his left leg, and he teetered precariously to that side, though he did not fall. The leaning saved him, however, as another gun flash burst out of the darkness. The bullet passed over him and hit a wood shutter over the only window in the kitchen. A hinge broke, and the shutter fell with a clatter, letting in a bit more light from the breaking dawn.

Calhoun had righted himself and focused on where the gunfire had come from. The extra light helped him identify his target. Buck Stover, whose arm was still bandaged from when Calhoun had wounded him back in Luster, was moving to his left. He fired again, and the lead ball clipped Calhoun's shirt collar.

Calhoun fired twice, hitting Stover high in the

chest and in the throat. Stover fell and twitched but otherwise didn't move. Calhoun shifted to his right as he heard the posse nearing the house, as well as men coming down the dilapidated stairs. He moved through a doorway into what appeared to be a sitting room, and went all the way to the back. He leaned against a wall in the far rear corner behind a sagging old chair.

As best he could tell, posse men were pouring into the kitchen and Laird's men were all downstairs. Pandemonium soon broke out in the kitchen, but it remained peaceful in the sitting room. Calhoun figured he would wait where he was until the outlaws and posse were through killing each other. Then he would finish up what needed doing. He could see no reason to wade into the midst of that chaos.

Within seconds, though, the shooting had shifted to outside. Men yelled and horses whinnied. There was galloping, and more shouts.

Marshal Sam Packard stepped into the sitting room, gun out and ready, and stopped a few steps in. His eyes searched the room. He spotted Calhoun, who had made no attempt to hide or go anywhere. "You're under arrest, Calhoun," he growled nastily. He had been too long on Calhoun's trail, had lost too many men, had seen no end of trouble, so he was in no mood to be civil to anyone, let alone the man who had caused him all the trouble.

Calhoun suddenly snapped a pistol up and fired three times. The first shot produced a dull clang; the second two smacked into flesh and bone.

Packard blanched, sure he was dead. He had

never seen anyone move so quickly, and it took him by surprise; he had thought he had the drop on Calhoun, since he had his revolver aimed roughly at the saddle tramp. He was even more surprised, though, that all three of Calhoun's shots had missed him. From what he had seen earlier of Calhoun's handiwork with a revolver, that was startling. Shaking a little from fear, nervousness, and relief, Packard was about to return fire, when something fell against him, almost knocking him down.

Packard glanced down at Royce Laird's body. There were two bloody holes in the outlaw leader's face. Confused, the marshal looked at Calhoun.

Calhoun was of more than half a mind to just shoot Packard and be done with it, but he could see no point to it. Not just yet anyway. "Drop your piece, Marshal," he said evenly. "Or I'll drop you."

Befuddled, Packard bent and set his pistol down carefully, lest it go off by accident. Then he straightened. He pointed to Laird's corpse, then waved a hand vaguely in Calhoun's direction. "Why?" he asked, still wondering just what was going on. "You had me dead to rights. You could've shot me and still have gotten Laird."

"I considered it," Calhoun said flatly. "Believe me. I figure I'm being a damn fool, but I decided to give you one last chance to see the truth."

The gunfire had stopped outside, and a couple of posse men ran into the sitting room. "You son of a bitch," Frankie Kitchell shouted, ready to plug Calhoun.

"Stop!" Packard bellowed, trying to regain at least some control over the situation.

"But Calhoun's about to . . ."

"He just shot Laird, who was about to put a bullet in my back," Packard snapped. "I owe him the right to speak his piece."

"You don't owe him a damn thing, Marshal," Kitchell snarled. He was standing mostly behind Packard, figuring he had some measure of protection that way.

"Shut up, Frankie," Packard said wearily. "Before I shoot you myself. Now go wait outside with the others."

"No, I'm gonna stay right here," Kitchell said adamantly. "Where I can keep an eye on that son of a bitch."

Packard gave up caring right at the moment. He whirled, lashing out. His fist caught Kitchell backhanded in the face.

Kitchell fell, finger jerking automatically on the trigger. Fortunately for all concerned, the bullet hit the far wall. Packard grabbed the young man's pistol in one hand and his shirt in the other. He hauled Kitchell to his feet, and jerked the revolver free.

"I am sick and tired of your horseshit, Frankie," Packard growled, heedless of the fact that Calhoun was behind him with a pistol still pointed at his back. "You've been a pain in my ass since we left Pecan Grove. Hell, since before that. You want my goddamn job, you can have it—when we get back to Pecan Grove. I ain't so sure you're gonna make it, though. Hell, I ain't so sure *I'm* gonna make it. Now get your ass outside and wait with the others."

"What about him?" Kitchell asked, face red from anger. He pointed to Calhoun.

"Depends on what he does," Packard said with a shrug. "He kills me, you're free to go after him yourself, if you've got the gumption." He shoved Kitchell away from him. "Now get!"

Kitchell and the other man, whom Calhoun did not know, shuffled out. Packard turned back to face Calhoun. He grinned a little lopsidedly by way of apology.

"What'm I gonna do with you, Marshal?" Calhoun asked. He was not smiling, of course, but his voice was calm and reasoned.

"That's your decision. But I thought you wanted me to see the truth."

"I've been tryin' to get you to see that since the Fullers were killed. I've told you all along I didn't kill 'em."

"Yeah, Laird killed 'em, right?" Packard countered a little sarcastically.

"Nope," Calhoun responded, surprising the lawman. "I thought he was behind it, but he wasn't. He knew about it, but he wasn't there. Sid Lockwood was the one who led that little escapade."

"Why?" Packard was unconvinced, but more willing to listen than he had been before, particularly since Calhoun had saved his life—and Laird had been ready to take it.

"Revenge against me," Calhoun said angrily, his rage at Lockwood renewed. "He was fit to be tied after I knocked the shit out of him in Hanney's. He found out I was stayin' with Mister and Miz Fuller. He picked a bunch of men and waited for his chance. Soon's as I left for Pecan Grove again, he rode in and killed them."

"How can you know that for sure?"

"One of the men who was along with Lockwood went to Pecan Grove afterward. He got drunk and flapped his gums while he was with Trude. I caught him after I escaped and took him out to the Fullers' place, where I encouraged him to talk. He told me what happened."

"Can you really believe the word of a man like that?"

Calhoun nodded. "When everything else fits into place I can. Go talk to Jethro Fuller. He'll tell you he found Marshal Buford wearin' one of his mother's necklaces."

"What . . . ?"

"Laird was Buford's wife's cousin. Buford told me so himself. I think Laird, or maybe Lockwood, gave him the necklace as payment for protectin' the gang."

"I ain't so sure . . ." Packard said. He was still skeptical, but was becoming convinced.

"I expect if you check over Laird and the others, you'll find some of the Fullers' personal effects."

Packard stood there wondering. He had hated Wade Calhoun right from the start, and wanted to believe the worst of him. He had seen Calhoun's kind before, and always loathed such men. They were a blight on any decent community. Those feelings had blinded him, he was beginning to think. He had simply refused to believe that Calhoun had told the truth about anything. The facts, though, had become almost so overwhelming that he could not in good conscience continue to consider Calhoun guilty of killing the Fullers.

"You've got a heap of other crimes to answer for, Calhoun," Packard said. He was rather disgusted with himself for not being able to just put this all to rest. It was obvious even to him now what the truth was; he just couldn't resist letting his personal feelings for Calhoun get in the way.

"Like what?"

"Knockin' me on the head."

"I didn't do that."

"All right," Packard conceded, "Dutch did it. It amounts to the same thing, since she did it to help you escape. Which is another thing you've got to answer for."

"I shouldn't've been locked up in the first place."

Packard shrugged. There was nothing he could do about that now. "Then there's a matter of horse theft. A hangin' offense if ever there was one. Goddammit, why'd you have to take *my* horse?"

"Thought it was the fair thing to do under the circumstances. You can have the horse back. Bockmeister's, too. I'll just take a couple of the outlaws' horses instead."

"I expect that'd be sort of fair," Packard said, mollified a little. "But what about all those men you killed? The men who rode with my posse?"

Calhoun shrugged. He felt only a little sorry for that; after all, they had been trying to kill him. "I gave you—and them—enough chances to back off. When you kept comin' after me, what was I supposed to do?"

"Surrender," Packard said flatly.

Calhoun simply snorted in response to that.

Packard nodded, knowing he had given a ridiculous response. "Well, what do we do now?" he asked.

"That's up to you, Marshal."

"Me?" Packard asked, startled. "You're the one's got the drop on me."

"You tell me you'll leave me be, and you're free to walk out of here."

"I could tell you that, and then have you arrested—or shot—when you're not expectin' it," Packard said. Not that he was really considering such a thing, though it was a possibility.

"You may be a fool at times, Marshal," Calhoun said evenly, "but I figure you're an honest man. You give me your word on it, and I'll not doubt you."

Packard looked at Calhoun suspiciously for some moments. "You're tellin' the truth, aren't you," he finally said.

"Yep. To me a man's word is inviolate."

Packard stood there thinking. There was no reason not to believe Calhoun about anything, including this last. The thought of having to go back to Pecan Grove, though, and explain to the wives and children of the men who had died on the posse that it had all been for naught, was not to his liking. That was the only thing staying him from doing what he knew he should. Then he shrugged mentally. He was a tough man, or at least he had used to be. He could face this adversity, just as he had faced so many troubles in the past.

Packard nodded. "Far's I'm concerned, Mister Calhoun, you're a free man," he said quietly. "You have my word on that."

"What about your other men?"

"You'll get no trouble from them. Except maybe Kitchell, who's an idiot."

"He tries something, he'll regret it," Calhoun said flatly.

"That's his problem." Packard paused. "One request, though?"

"What's that?"

"I'd be mighty obliged if you were to keep your distance from Pecan Grove. Forever."

Calhoun nodded.

# CHAPTER

# 22

"Pick up your weapon, Marshal," Calhoun said quietly.

Packard looked at him, surprised anew. Then he nodded and knelt. He picked up his revolver, uncocked it, and holstered it. He touched Laird's chest to make sure there was really no life left in the outlaw leader. He didn't think there could be, not with the two bullets in the face and brain. He was a little startled when he encountered something hard. He pulled Laird's shirt open a little ways. "I'll be damned," he said, voice showing a little humor for the first time in quite a while. "Royce is wearin' some old armor, like the Spaniards used to wear. Or so I've heard tell they did."

Calhoun hurried over, also knelt and checked it out. "That's from the Fullers' house," he said, looking across the corpse at Packard. "Jess told me he dug it up in a field some years back. He had it hangin' on the wall. When I went back after escapin', I thought somethin' was missin' from the house, but I just couldn't place it. This was what it was, though. Sure as shit."

Packard stared at Calhoun. There was no good in denying that Laird's men—at least some of them—were the ones who had killed Jess and Millie Fuller. He was even having a hard time disliking Calhoun anymore. Oh, he still thought Calhoun was a bloodthirsty, troublemaking so and so, but he couldn't actually hate him.

"Well," Packard said, rising, "let's go see what the damage is." He was not thrilled with the idea. He was sure he had lost more men. The only question was how many. And how many outlaws they had killed.

"There's a pretty good reward on Laird, I reckon," Calhoun said, also standing. "If I was you, I'd take the body back to Luster or somewhere else and get the money on him."

"I'm not in this for blood money, Mister Calhoun," Packard said stiffly.

"That money could help ease the grief of the families of the men who got killed," Calhoun said quietly.

"Now that's a reason for takin' a reward," Packard said after only a moment's hesitation. "Don't you want your share, though? Hell, after all, you were the one who killed him."

"Don't need it," Calhoun lied. Actually, he knew he could use the money. Trouble was, he didn't want it. He had nothing against taking bounty money, but this time, he wanted nothing more than to pay back all of Laird's men for what they had done to the Fullers. That was all.

Packard shrugged. It was none of his concern, and it meant more money for him and his men. He headed out into the kitchen area, stepping over the body of one of his men. He saw Buck Stover's corpse in the corner, plus the body of someone he didn't know near the door leading to the outside. That one was a boy's, not more than sixteen.

"I expect there'll be others upstairs," Calhoun said, pointing to the youth's corpse.

Packard nodded again. He walked outside, followed by Calhoun. "Well, boys, what's the . . . ?" He stopped when he saw Dutch Trude and Fuller sitting on an old log bench. Both were bound and gagged. He had a sudden jolt of fear as he realized that in a second or two Calhoun was going to see it, too. "What the hell's the meaning of this?" he managed to get out before Calhoun could say anything. He pointed to Dutch Trude and Fuller.

"I arrested 'em," Kitchell said proudly. His smirk was directed at both Packard and Calhoun.

"What in hell for?" Packard demanded.

"I thought you'd want it that way," Kitchell said, words sounding as if he thought Packard was an idiot.

"You ain't supposed to think, you dumb bastard," Packard snapped. He was enraged that Kitchell would take such a thing upon himself.

"But I . . ." The smirk was gone from Kitchell's face, replaced by an annoyed look that bordered on anger.

"Don't 'but' me, goddammit," Packard snarled. "Unloose those two people right goddamn now."

"I will not," Kitchell said stiffly. "If you're not gonna do your job, someone has to."

"Don't you tell me my job, you . . ."

Calhoun shoved Packard out of the way and limped forward a few steps. He had a Dragoon in his hand. It was cocked, and aimed at Kitchell's head. "Let 'em loose, boy. Now!" Calhoun said in low, deadly tones.

"You think you're a pretty big man when you've got the advantage on someone. Same as last time. You put that gun away, and we'll just see how tough you really are."

"Let those two loose, and I'll give you your chance, boy," Calhoun said evenly. He was not concerned in the least with a cocky blowhard like Frankie Kitchell.

Kitchell glared, as if ready to argue. Then he saw the look in Calhoun's cool eyes. He turned and swiftly undid the ropes holding Dutch Trude and Fuller, and then untied the old bandanna gags. He faced Calhoun again. "Now what do you say, you yellow-bellied bug?" he asked arrogantly.

Calhoun eased the hammer of the Dragoon down and slid the pistol away. "Your call, boy. Pistols? Fists?"

"Fists, I think. That's how you beat me the last time—when I wasn't ready for you. Now I'm gonna show you how it feels to get clobbered in front of a bunch of people."

"Have at it, asshole," Calhoun said evenly.

Kitchell swaggered forward, flexing shoulder and arm muscles. He was a well-built, strong young man, and he knew it. He balled his fists and kept advancing, wondering a little why Calhoun was making no move to defend himself. He threw a tentative punch.

Calhoun flicked out his left arm, easily blocking

the blow. He did the same twice more, as Kitchell tested him. Then Kitchell swung a hard left at Calhoun's stomach. Or maybe his groin. Calhoun half turned, catching the punch near the kidney. He jerked his right elbow backward.

Kitchell's feeling of satisfaction at landing the punch was momentary, as he caught the elbow in the cheekbone. It knocked him down.

Calhoun turned slowly and waited for Kitchell to get up. Then he slammed three hard punches in rapid succession into Kitchell's stomach and ribs. Kitchell groaned and sagged. Calhoun spun him and then shoved him forward.

Kitchell slammed into and snapped one of the rickety braces for the porch roof, which fell, partly on Kitchell. Kitchell was on the ground wondering just what had happened, and getting really frightened for the first time. He rolled over onto his seat and looked at Calhoun. It was hard to breathe, and he knew he had no chance of beating Calhoun. He went for his pistol.

Calhoun pulled a Dragoon and fired, hitting Kitchell low in the stomach.

Kitchell yelled, then looked with dazed eyes at Calhoun. "You shot me," he said, seemingly surprised by the fact.

"Yep," Calhoun said, walking up, kneeling, and taking Kitchell's pistol. He pitched the weapon out of the way. "Down low in the gut, too. It's gonna take you a while to die, and it'll hurt like all hellfire."

"You son of a . . ." Kitchell sucked in a breath as pain roared through him. He moaned and then began to cry.

Calhoun turned away and walked back to Packard. He waved a hand around. "Don't look like your boys did too well," he said.

Packard shook his head. The only bodies of outlaws around were those killed by Wade Calhoun. The marshal was glad, though, that only the one man inside—and now Kitchell—had been killed. He had been fairly sure that he was going to lose nearly all his men once the fighting had started. "Well, they ain't like you and me, you know," he offered as a feeble defense.

Calhoun nodded.

"Well, what're you plannin' to do now, Wade?" Packard asked.

"Go after the rest of those bastards. Hell, Lockwood was the one who caused all this trouble. There's no way he's gonna get away."

"You leavin' straight off?"

Calhoun nodded. "Soon's I can get my leg bandaged up and my saddle moved."

"Anything I can do for you?"

Calhoun stood in thought for a moment, then nodded again. "Take Mister Fuller with you. I was about to send him back to his family, but Trude was afraid you might arrest him again. Or that Comanches might get him."

"That wouldn't be good."

"Nope."

"He can go with us, sure," Packard said with a nod. "Won't be no trouble at all." He paused. "How about Dutch? We can take her along, too, if you like."

"I'd rather kiss the devil's ass on Main Street in

Pecan Grove than to leave Vade now," Dutch Trude said defiantly.

Packard looked at Calhoun, who shrugged and said, "You heard the lady."

Packard nodded. He turned and yelled, "Page, you and the rest of the boys start burying the unfortunate folks from the house. Our men, too. The outlaws you can sling over horses and we'll take 'em with us."

Dutch Trude walked over to Calhoun and took his arm. "Come on, Vade, sit on the bench. I'll try to fix your leg some."

"Try?" Calhoun asked suspiciously as he hobbled toward the old bench.

"Yah. I don't know much about these things."

"Maxwell knows some herb medicines and the like," Packard said, walking up. "You want him to take a look?"

Calhoun looked at Dutch Trude, whose eyes clouded angrily for a moment. Then she smiled and nodded.

Minutes later Butch Maxwell arrived in front of Calhoun. He had a small bag of herbs and roots and such. In a very short time, he had concocted some kind of poultice and slapped it on the wound, after making sure the bullet had not stayed in the leg. Then he wrapped it with cloth Dutch Trude had found in the house. "Dampen that poultice of a time," Maxwell said, standing and beginning to put away his things. "And make it fresh every day or so."

Calhoun nodded. "I'm obliged, Mister Maxwell." He knew the posse man was not pleased with having had to help him.

Maxwell shrugged and went to help his fellows.

"Well, Trude," Calhoun said, standing, "I'd best go change my saddle over. Marshal Packard'd like his horse back. I am a mite surprised, though, that the horse and saddle are still here, as much as those outlaws must've wanted to get away from here."

"Jethro and I saw the posse heading this vay, and ve figured all hell vas goink to break loose anytime. So ve rode over here and got the horse and saddle avay. Ve brought him back vhen ve saw that the fightink vas over."

"I'm obliged to you, too," Calhoun said solemnly. He stopped at the corral and looked at the few horses left in there. He decided on Laird's big sorrel gelding. It took a little effort to quiet the horse and get a rope around him, but then the animal was quite docile as Calhoun saddled him.

"Ready?" Calhoun asked, looking at Dutch Trude. When she nodded, both mounted and rode to where Packard was standing, talking with Maxwell.

Packard looked up. "You know where they're going?" he asked.

"More or less. You know where a place called Branchwater is?"

"Eight, ten miles that way," Packard said, pointing to the northwest. "It ain't much of a place."

"Don't matter, as long as what I'm lookin' for is there," Calhoun said flatly.

"Good huntin', then, Mister Calhoun. But mind that favor I asked."

Calhoun nodded.

"Put a bullet into Lockwood for me," Fuller said, walking up. He had thought to argue about going back home with the posse, but had decided he'd had enough of fighting and bloodshed. He wanted to be home with his family and tend to his farm. He wanted to get to his parents' house and see what was what there. He had many things to do, and none involved spending any more time tracking down outlaws.

"I'll do that."

"Thanks for all you've done for me," Fuller said. "Especially after the way I felt about you at the start."

"Wasn't much," Calhoun said. He leaned over and held out Packard's revolver, the one he had taken quite some time ago. When Packard took the weapon, Calhoun turned his horse's head and rode off. A moment later, Dutch Trude was riding alongside him.

They stopped less than a mile away for some jerky and water, and so Calhoun could clean his weapons. He hated having dirty guns. His pistols were what had kept him alive all this time, and dirty ones would almost certainly misfire when he needed them most. Because of that, he was almost obsessive about cleaning them.

# CHAPTER

# ★ 23 ★

Branchwater was a dusty, windswept hellhole, and Calhoun wondered why anyone would live in such a godforsaken place. The adobe and sod buildings were dilapidated and half seemed to be falling down. Several sections of the town had only blackened remains from a large fire. Dust blew unimpeded through the nearly deserted streets. The heat baked everything to a fine, crackling hardness. It was just after noon, and there was not a cloud to break the sparkling blueness of the sky, or dent the sun's fearsome heat.

Calhoun could feel more than see people peering out from behind shutters or curtains. There were almost no women or children, as far as Calhoun could tell, which didn't surprise him in such a place. The few people on the street hurriedly headed indoors when they saw Calhoun entering the festering boil of a town.

Calhoun and Dutch Trude stopped when they saw Sid Lockwood, 'Fuss Connover, The Pole, and Mike Ferguson step out of a poor excuse for a saloon and move into the middle of the street. Calhoun handed his reins to Dutch Trude. "Stay here," he ordered as he dismounted.

"You still got that pistol we took from Paulie Goodrich?" he asked, looking up at Dutch Trude.

"Yah." She patted the deep pocket of her dress.

"Keep it handy," Calhoun said. He got his two Colt Walkers from the saddle holsters. He stuck one of the two big pistols into his belt at the back. The other remained in his right hand. Then he turned and limped up the street to where the four outlaws were waiting for him. As he walked, he thought Branchwater, being the hellhole at the end of nowhere that it was, was a fitting place to finish this trouble.

The wind increased some, whipping along the dusty streets, tugging at his shirtsleeves and hat. A few tumbleweeds rolled swiftly down the street, propelled by the low-whistling wind.

Calhoun never stopped. When he was about twenty feet away from the four outlaws, he brought the Walker up and began firing.

Connover was the first to go down, two lead balls in his chest. He had just enough time before he died to show surprise at the sudden open firing. For some reason, he had thought that Calhoun would give him and his companions a chance to draw before shooting. He didn't know why he had thought that, since he would've done just what Calhoun had.

Calhoun took out Connover first because he was closest. He shot Ferguson next, since he figured an old hand like Ferguson was one of the two most dangerous men he faced—Lockwood being the other. But he wanted to save Lockwood for last, if he could, to make the man suffer the most for his cold-blooded killing of Jess and Millie Fuller.

Ferguson didn't even get his pistol out of his holster before he was writhing on the ground with two bullets in his guts.

The other two outlaws hastily and rather belatedly yanked out their weapons and began firing away at Calhoun. The saddle tramp ignored their gunfire.

Calhoun fired the fifth ball in his Walker and then tossed the weapon into the dust. He grabbed the other from his belt and continued firing.

The Pole got off two shots before he, too, fell. But the big, bull-necked man got back up. He didn't look too steady, but he came up firing.

When he saw The Pole drop, Calhoun had turned his attention to Lockwood. He'd winged the outlaw in the gun arm with one shot, and then shot him in the leg, and then in the other arm.

Suddenly a ball creased Calhoun's side, and he spun, partly from the bullet's impact, partly from anger. He was winged again, this time in the leg, only inches from the wound he'd suffered earlier in the day. The leg gave out on him and he fell. The Pole fired again. Calhoun heard a horse squeal and he cranked his head around to see Dutch Trude's horse go down, apparently fully on top of her.

"Shit," he muttered, heart sinking. There was no

way Dutch Trude could have lived through that. Not with the way the horse had gone down atop her. He wanted to rush over there, perhaps hold her for a moment, but he could not face that right now. As fearless as he was, that would be too much for him until his other business was finished. Only then would he be able to steel himself to his loss. In a fit of rage, he shoved to his feet, firing his Walker. It emptied in moments, and he tossed it away. Ripping out a Dragoon, he blasted The Pole five times, each lead ball smashing into the outlaw's big chest.

The Pole fell, sending up a cloud of dust. He writhed and twitched, but this time he did not get up.

Calhoun dropped the empty Dragoon into the holster and pulled the other. With deadly intent in his eyes, he walked toward Lockwood, who lay in a puddle of his own blood.

Lockwood had tried getting up, but he could put no weight on his shattered arms, so he had given that idea up. Instead, he tried to cock his pistol, but that, too, was proving to be more than he could do with his bullet-broken arms.

"Goddamn, if you ain't a miserable excuse for a man," Calhoun taunted as he loomed over Lockwood. "Chickenshit, back-shootin' little bastard."

"Who the hell *are* you?" Lockwood asked, eyes clouded with pain and wonder.

"Name's Wade Calhoun. You know that. I'm a friend—was a friend—to Jess and Millie Fuller."

"And now you're their self-appointed avenger, eh?"

Calhoun nodded.

"Well, then, go to hell, Mister Avenger."

Calhoun placed a boot heel on the wound in one of Lockwood's arms and pushed down. He ground his heel hard, as if trying to stamp out a giant cigarette butt.

Lockwood hissed in pain and the already shattered bone splintered some more.

Calhoun looked around. People were still watching from doorways and windows, but no one seemed interested in bothering him. He dropped the Dragoon into the holster and rolled a cigarette. After lighting it, he dropped the still burning match onto Lockwood's shirt.

"Son of a bitch!" Lockwood snapped. He went to sweep away the match and gasped as pain lanced through his arm.

"There ain't a way I can think of to make you suffer enough for what you done, boy," Calhoun said, voice raspy with rage. "But I aim to see you suffer some." He kicked Lockwood in the wounded leg.

When he finished his cigarette—and ground it out on Lockwood's forehead—Calhoun picked up the outlaw's revolver. He knelt and began cracking Lockwood's bones, one at a time, with the pistol butt. First a rib or two, then a shinbone; a couple more ribs, than a few fingers.

Lockwood screamed steadily as Calhoun hammered him slowly to pulp. The screams eventually began to fade as the pain so overwhelmed Lockwood that he teetered on the edge of unconsciousness.

When Calhoun saw that, he eased off a bit. As Lockwood started to come around, Calhoun carefully cracked Lockwood's cheekbones and jaw, then the orbit bones around the eyes.

Finally Calhoun rose. He dropped the pistol and bent. Grabbing Lockwood by the shirtfront, he lifted him a little off the ground. Then he began bouncing him up and down.

Lockwood screamed a few times, then passed out. Calhoun dropped the broken thing. Angry still, Calhoun grabbed Lockwood's pistol again, and fired the last three shots in it, two into one thigh, the third into the other. Then he tossed the pistol into the dust, turned, and retrieved his own discarded weapons.

With a last look at the shattered outlaw, who was not yet dead, but who would never live, Calhoun turned and headed, limping seriously, toward his horse—and the one lying on Dutch Trude. His heart was heavy.

Calhoun was as surprised as he could be when he neared the horse and heard Dutch Trude muttering, mostly in German, but with a few English curse words thrown in here and there for good measure. He hurried and saw Dutch Trude trying to pull her leg out from under the almost dead horse.

"You ain't dead," he said, feeling rather stupid at having uttered what was so obvious.

"No, I'm not dead. Now get me out of here!"

"Yes'm." Calhoun shot the horse in the head, then hauled up on the saddle as hard as he could.

It was enough to allow Dutch Trude to get her trapped foot out. She stood, gingerly testing it.

"You all right?" Calhoun asked.

"Yah. I think so." She smiled. "Goot enough, I suppose."

Calhoun nodded. He climbed onto his horse and held out a hand. Dutch Trude grabbed it, and allowed Calhoun to pull her up onto the horse behind him. "Where to?" he asked.

"Anyvhere but Pecan Grove."

Calhoun touched his spurs to the horse's sides, and they rode out of Branchwater.

CLINT HAWKINS is the pseudonym of a newspaper editor and writer who lives in Phoenix, Arizona.

# HarperPaperbacks *By Mail*

**Experience sizzling suspense in the breathtaking Southwest by *New York Times* bestselling author**

## TONY HILLERMAN

Master of suspense Tony Hillerman weaves Native American tradition into multi-layered mysteries featuring Officer Jim Chee and Lt. Joe Leaphorn of the Navajo Tribal Police. Brimming with rich detail and relentless excitement, each of his eleven gripping mysteries defy being put down before the very last page is turned

### THE BLESSING WAY

Lt. Joe Leaphorn must stalk a supernatural killer known as the "Wolf-Witch" along a chilling trail of mysticism and murder.

### THE DARK WIND

Sgt. Jim Chee becomes trapped in a deadly web of a cunningly spun plo driven by Navajo sorcer and white man's greed.

### COYOTE WAITS

When a bullet kills Officer Jim Chee's good friend Del, a Navajo shaman is arrested for homicide, but the case is far from closed.

### THE GHOSTWAY

A photo sends Officer Chee on an odyssey of murder and revenge that moves from an Indian hogan to a deadly healing ceremony.

### DANCE HALL OF THE DEAD

An archeological dig, a steel hypodermic needle, and the strange laws of the Zuni complicate the disappearance of two young boys.

### LISTENING WOMAN

A baffling investigation of murder, ghosts and witches can only be solved by Lt. Leaphorn, a man who understands both his own people an cold-blooded killers.